MEG DAILEY

A HORDE OF DEAD POETS

SOME RAIN MUST FALL

MEG DAILEY

Percy's Heart Press www.percysheartpress.com

Publisher's Note: This is a work of fiction. Names, characters, places, and incidents are a product of the author's imagination. Locales and public names are sometimes used for atmospheric purposes. Any resemblance to actual people, living or dead, or to businesses, companies, events, institutions, or locales is completely coincidental.

Book Layout

Edited by Carla Lewis, Jess Moore

Cover Art and Design © 2024 Adina Chiles

Interior Formatting by Book Savvy Services

Credit to: Longfellow, Henry Wadsworth. "The Rainy Day", *Ballads and Other Poems*, 1842

Content Warning; Depictions of Suicide.

*To everyone over the years who asked me when I'd finally
publish something. It's now! I hope this is worth the wait.*

The day is cold, and dark, and dreary
    It rains, and the wind is never weary;
    The vine still clings to the mouldering wall,
    But at every gust the dead leaves fall,
    And the day is dark and dreary.

My life is cold, and dark, and dreary;
    It rains, and the wind is never weary;
    My thoughts still cling to the mouldering Past,
    But the hopes of youth fall thick in the blast,
    And the days are dark and dreary.

Be still, sad heart! and cease repining;
    Behind the clouds is the sun still shining;
    Thy fate is the common fate of all,
    Into each life some rain must fall,
    Some days must be dark and dreary.

Henry Wadsworth Longfellow
"The Rainy Day"

Contents

Prologue

SUNDAY NIGHT

I take one squishy step onto my doormat, turned practically to mush by the rain. My boot slips before I can get the other foot down, and the kitchen knife flies from my hand as I fumble to catch myself. It lands on the stone of my doorstep with a clatter, the dull metal reflecting a duller version of the already dull gray skies above.

For a second, I imagine having fallen forward, holding the knife just so, and watching my own blood pool across the ground.

The thought would be morbid and intrusive if it wasn't essentially the reason I'm out here anyway.

I pull the door closed behind me with a solid *click*. I don't bother locking it. I won't be back, so someone will need to be able to get inside to go through my stuff, and no one else has a key.

I could have given Callie a key.

I wish I had.

I'm glad I didn't.

My hand shakes as I reach for the knife, now slick with

both cool rain and warm sweat. The handle feels insubstantial, ineffective for what I'm about to do, but I know the blade is strong enough. Stainless steel and oiled, the kind of implement you can't even put in the dishwasher without ruining it. The handle is almost flimsy in comparison, like it has no business holding something so sharp and deadly. Neither do I, really, but hey, here I am.

I take another step, off the stoop and into the mud. My foot sinks half an inch, and I wince, thinking about how difficult it's going to be to get the muck out of the crevices later.

But I guess I won't have to worry about that.

That one step is all it takes to bring me out from under the awning and into the dripping rain. It's not pouring in great globs or drizzling in a mist; it's drips and drops, enough to start soaking in right away. Behind me, the house looms dark under hazy clouds. The leaves on the long vines creeping along the outer wall, once vibrant green and now brown and drooping, twitch as the rain hits them, like they're waving goodbye.

It's been raining for ages. It seems like it hasn't stopped since summer ended. As if to emphasize the point, my shoes sink a tiny bit more when I shift my weight. Have to keep moving.

I'm not going to die here.

Another three squelching steps are all it takes to get me to the tree line, where my boots immediately stop sinking and instead settle unsteadily onto inches, feet, miles of dead leaves. My footsteps go silent. All I can hear is my own deep breathing, measured as though each might be my last, and the susurrus of rain. Rain on leaves, on bark, landing in self-made puddles and sinking into the back of the cozy sweater I put on this morning, which is getting heavier by the second. I feel slow, like I'm wading through a lake. It's muggy and warmer than usual for fall, and the wet heat chokes me. I might drown before I get where I'm going.

But that would defeat the purpose entirely, and I can't let that happen. So I force myself to breathe, to keep moving forward. Ten more steps. Twenty. Counting up instead of down, because that feels less ominous. I grip the knife to center myself.

The first ever knives are thought to have been made of obsidian, volcano glass. *That* would have been a properly witchy knife, something to make sure the spells went right—the ones that involved cutting, anyway. Could lava glass go in the dishwasher, though?

The silvery blade of my modern-day stainless practically blends in with the haze of the day. If I turn it in my hand, it seems to almost disappear.

I distract myself with this minor magic trick as I walk, as if maybe, if I'm not paying attention, if I don't think too hard about it, I can avoid what comes next.

But I know I can't. I've tried avoiding it plenty recently, and it's not working.

So, this has to work instead.

I can't keep living like this.

I'm at the tree before I know it.

My feet could carry me here through driving snow or darkest night—like some kind of sick, haunted mail service. I would know this path if I were deaf, blind, or numb. If my legs stopped working, I could crawl here on my belly like a worm searching for food.

I've tried to get lost in these woods plenty of times. Even as a kid, when my family lived here and I knew little else of the world, I knew I could find my way around these trees. Unlike some forests that refuse to let people go, this one has never seemed to want to keep me too long. No matter how far I walk, which direction I take, I eventually end up back on my front stoop.

Or here. At this tree.

As far as I know, this tree is nothing special to anyone but me. It might have been tall once, before a lightning strike or another tree took it down. Now it's a tall stump, hollow in the middle, and what's left of it forms a sort of arch that stretches to the ground. Until a few years ago, I was short enough to walk under it, and I had to climb quite a bit to sit on top. Now I can touch the crown of the arch with one hand reaching—though I do still have to climb to get up there. I'm taller but not sprier, unfortunately.

I used to be out here all the time before my last birthday. That arch makes a pretty damn comfortable bench, the perfect spot to sit and breathe and think. I'd play "I Spy" with birds, catch leaves as they fluttered down from the distant boughs and press them into my notebooks, and watch squirrels bury their treasures for winter around the roots.

A small mound of dirt squats right under the top of the arch, freshly turned, damp but still standing.

I buried something here too.

I don't know what. Whenever I try to remember, my mind goes all blurry, like going back over a dream too long after waking up. I can almost see the shape of it, but more than that, I can feel that it's something I don't *want* to see. I'm afraid of it.

I must have forgotten for a reason. You don't block something out of your own memory for no reason. But that's not why I'm here now, so I roll my eyes away from the dirt and back up to the arch.

I square my shoulders. I breathe.

"You know why I'm here."

I quickly glance around. Nothing moves except the rain, falling in a curtain, hemming me in.

"You have to stop this. I don't know what you are, but I know it's me you want. I'm here now. So take me."

Still nothing. No shadows, no eyes, no—

A bird flits across my vision, sending my heart pounding double-time. When it's out of sight, I turn in a slow circle, sure I'll see something terrifying right behind me.

But there's still nothing.

Just as I expected. Talking won't be enough.

"Fine!" I shout into the gray. "You think I'm scared? I'm not. Not of you, and not of this."

Before I can think better of it, I grasp the knife in both hands, swing up, and plunge it down into my chest.

It's weird, how I can feel it go in, feel it move through me, feel the pinch of pain and cold of metal through fabric and flesh. I see myself hit the ground, mud and leaves splashing into my eyes as I fall. Bitter mud sloshes into my gaping mouth. Then I can finally hear something other than the rain as my own last breath comes wheezing out before it all goes black.

Christopher Lee was right.

I OPEN MY EYES TO DARKNESS.

It's familiar—pretty much in the job description that a necromancer always has to have one foot on the other side of the Veil—but usually, I'm looking from a distance, leaning in for a brief peek or pulling it open to let someone through.

For a moment, I'm relieved. It worked.

But then . . .

"Fuck!" I sit up abruptly, and the wound in my chest aches in protest. If I breathe deeply, I can still feel the steel, cold and scraping, even though I can't see it here. It's still in my body. And if I can still feel my body, I'm not all the way gone.

"No! You were supposed to take me, just do it! Why am I still here?"

I stare into the abyss and see it: the shadow within the shadows, the monster from my childhood nightmares and adulthood daydreams. I can't quite make out its shape. My mind is making something up to make sense of what I'm not seeing, like ducks in a dark, damp cave.

Then the eyes appear. White, but not a bright light—white like a distant, dying star, something impossibly far away even though it appears to be only a few feet from me.

The eyes blink slowly, cat-like. But the shadow doesn't speak.

It never does. *Bitch*.

"Isn't this what you wanted?" I ask desperately, pressing an arm to my throbbing middle. "Why else would you have been following me all these months? You wanted the dead girl dead, and here she is. Let me out of here so I can die already."

The eyes, initially just specks of light, elongate and go sideways, and my mind supplies the image of a head being tilted.

"Why?" I demand, nearly out of breath. Is that a good sign? Is my body letting go? I know the answer, but I don't want to admit it. I know how it feels when a soul goes entirely, and this isn't it.

Blink.

Blink.

"I did it again." Shifting, I pull my knees to my chest. "I disappointed them. I . . . hurt them. And this is all I can do now. All I have left to give. I know that."

It's my own fault this thing has been wreaking havoc on my life. My work, my family, Aaron, Callie . . . god. If it hurt Callie, I would never forgive myself.

I want it to hurt me instead.

I slam my fists on the nonexistent ground. There's no pain, but my breastbone gives an answering lurch.

"Get it over with already! Let me go and fuck back off to wherever you came from!"

The ache in my chest ramps up suddenly, sending me curling into a ball. The void of the floor feels like nothing. The pain feels like everything.

Finally.

And then it's gone.

Shit.

If I can feel the pain this acutely, then I'm definitely not going to die. It's not going to let me. It's going to put me back, to torture me more, to torture them. But why? I don't understand, if this isn't the solution, then what—

"Don't—!"

Blink.

I smell rain. I taste mud.

I open my eyes to a curtain of gray.

Almost immediately, my eyes blur with moisture—tears or rain or both. Then I take a deep breath and feel . . . nothing.

A flex of my right hand confirms the plastic knife handle is still gripped in it tightly. With my left, I reach up and tentatively pat my sternum, running my fingers across the unblemished front of my sweater.

Thank fuck, I think suddenly, feeling more relieved at this than I had at my first fresh breath. *I love this sweater.*

Then, just to be sure, I plunge my hand up under the sweater, gasping at the chill of a cold touch on my warm stomach, and let my pruned fingers skitter over the damp skin above my ribs, just under my bra.

There. A small scar, about the size of a kitchen knife blade.

I did it.

I failed.

Shit, shit, SHIT.

With all the strength I have—which is more than I should have, given I've just come back from the brink of death—I haul myself into a sitting position, then let go of the knife long enough to push myself roughly to my feet.

I look at the blade for a long while. Clean. Bloodless. As is the ground under my feet, not a single speck on a single leaf, even though I must have bled quite a bit. The steel landed at the right angle to catch the last of the light falling through the diminished canopy of the fall-ridden trees. It shines against the dark, drippy, muddy background on which it lays.

With a sigh, I bend to pick it up. "Leave no trace" and all that.

My footsteps on the way back to the house are silent.

Even the whispering of the rain seems to have died down, though it hasn't stopped. It feels like it will never stop.

Neither will I, I promise myself, adjusting the knife handle in my grip.

I have to try something else. Anything else.

I can't let it hurt more people.

There has to be another way.

The leafy vines are still waving as I approach the house, as if they're mocking me for failing. I really ought to cut them down. They'll attract wasps in the summer if I don't.

Problems for future-me. Present-me can't be bothered.

I push open the front door, take one step inside, and immediately go sliding across the floor, leaving a muddy trail in my wake. I barely manage to catch myself on the breakfast nook in the middle of the room, stopping my own fall but sending the knife flying across the counter and onto the floor near the fridge. I glare down at my boots in dismay.

It seems I will have to worry about the mud in the crevices after all.

PART ONE

Cold, Dark, and Dreary

One

MONDAY MORNING

The next morning, I wake groggy as hell and with an ache in my abdomen but not much else to show for my wild night out. It's probably for the best that I didn't dream. My dreams can get vivid, and if I'm particularly tired, I'm prone to sleep paralysis. Thankfully, I haven't had an episode in the six months I've been cursed. I don't know what I'd do if I had to face the shadow monster of my nightmares while tired *and* paralyzed.

I drag myself out of bed one limb at a time, arms flopping over my body to propel my torso up as my feet reluctantly meet the floor. I take a moment to wiggle my bare toes in the soft rug. It's almost enough to lure me back into bed, the reminder of soft comfort. But alas. If I'm not dead, I have to go to work.

Shouldn't have tried to die on a Sunday, I chide myself. *Oh well.*

As if I hadn't tried to escape it, my schedule runs through my head: check in; set up my crystal ball and tarot cards on the table at the back of the shop; settle behind the curtain that pretends at privacy while I conjure the dead for the living to chat with.

I've talked to Miss Tess about adding an actual room, a truly closed off space for me to do my work. I've even made the argument that it would be better for the ambiance. After all, a medium is only as good as the aesthetics she calls on—because the ghosts she calls on can't always be bothered. Miss Tess—correctly—made the counterargument that what I really wanted was a place to hide out from wandering customers, lest I must speak to the living more than necessary. And then she said no and shooed me back to my curtain.

Curtains may be temporary, but forced customer service lasts forever.

My mouth tastes of mud, so I brush my teeth and tongue twice. My hair is matted, leaves still stuck behind my ears, and I rush through a quick shower, too hot and too short, and watch the evidence of my misadventure in the woods swirl down the drain.

As I step out of the shower, I catch a glimpse of myself in the mirror and nearly fall backward into the tub.

Fuck, I look spooky. Which is normally part of the ambiance—black hair long enough to drape dramatically into my eyes and skin so pale I could pass for a ghost myself half the time, really makes for a good show in the right lighting—but Christ alive, could I not jump scare myself please?

My not-quite-death has me off-kilter.

Once I've settled from the scare of seeing myself, I spot the shadow in the corner of the room, watching from behind the wall that hides my toilet. It shifts slightly, and I flinch again. I try to ignore it as I do my makeup, but as soon as I lean in and bring the eyeliner pencil to my eye, the shadow darts toward me, and the glass of the mirror cracks. I jump back half a second before the shadow makes contact, and glittering glass rains down into the sink and vanity with a sound like bells, if bells were tailor-made to rip you to shreds.

Well. Fuck.

I step as carefully as I can around the sharp, shining obstacle course, then dust my feet off once I'm clear, just in case. There's no time to clean that mess up now, but luckily I live alone, so it won't be a danger to anyone else until I get back.

I shuffle back to my room to quickly do my eyeliner in the small plastic mirror on my dresser and pull on my outfit for the day. My dark socks and long black dress stick to me in the places I don't have time to dry, and my hair—that'll get taken care of on the ride. Assuming it isn't raining still.

Halfway through lacing up one boot, I glance out the window.

Yeah, it's still raining.

It's always fucking raining.

Downstairs, I snatch my cross-shoulder work bag off the couch a little too quickly, and my tarot deck slips out through the battered zipper along the top, spilling across the couch and floor, a prophetic game of 78 pickup.

"Wow, rude," I scold the cards as if they did it on purpose. As I scoop them up and pack them more securely into a pocket inside the bag, I wonder who will be getting the influence of my family's twenty-year-old couch in their reading today.

I could leave most of this stuff at work if I wanted, but I've always been a little protective of my gear—my cards, my crystal ball, my favorite lavender-scented incense sticks and the gryphon-shaped burner I set them in. Even the non-magic pieces are special to me, especially the Zippo Callie got me for my birthday last year: it's silver and has stars engraved on every side. Very good for the ambiance. I grab a poncho and throw it on over the bag, which hangs in a blob right above my hip.

Outside, it's drizzling more than full-on raining, which is a relief, at least until I start moving.

My bike leans against the house, the pale blue of its paint just about matching the faded blue of the siding. It would almost blend right into the wall if not for the dark slashes of the rubber handles and the darker circles denoting the tires. I've never had a car of my own. I can drive—when the house was still my parents', they'd send me out on errands occasionally in their car—but the few trips I take these days that require more than a bike can be done in Aaron's car. Plus, cars cost money, which I can't say I have in spades right now.

As I'm wheeling the bike away from the house, movement in the trees catches my eye, and I whirl, the handles nearly sliding right out of my hands.

A squirrel darts up the tree, away from me.

"Oh, fuck off," I mutter, shaking myself.

I'd say I'm just being afraid of my own shadow, but I'm not sure how literal of a description that is. I still don't know what's following me, but I wish more than anything that it would stop.

If it was a ghost, it would be a piece of cake for me to get rid of it. As a medium—the ghosts-only kind of necromancer —poking through the Veil to pull souls through or push them back is my specialty. I've been doing it since I was ten. I can tell when it's a soul refusing to go—the three up in my attic, for example, won't budge an inch. They were there long before me, and I wouldn't be surprised if they were there long after me too.

But this shadow thing? It's not like them. At least those three I can feel, the presence of a soul like a cold spot in a warm bath. I've only ever felt two things when I tried to touch the shadow: hot, searing pain or nothing at all.

I'm not sure which is worse, to be honest. Nothing should feel like nothing.

I pedal away as fast as I can make my tires go in the muck, hoping I don't see anyone else on the way into town. That would be my luck, to be tired, wet, *and* late because I got accosted on the one road to and from my house.

Today, though, the road seems to be blessedly empty— probably because it is cursedly muddy as fuck. My treads eat up the distance anyway, so, small blessings.

It's a relief to finally hit the paved road that leads into town. Nothing beats the smell of petrichor off a road on a warm day. Today is chilly, all of last night's heavy heat having dissipated, but the smell tickles my nose anyway, teasing warmer weather.

It feels like we haven't seen the sun in weeks. Months, maybe. Summer showers bring May flowers, but cold fall showers just bring gloom.

At least I'll be able to use that gloom at work.

Ambiance.

Two

By the time I get to the shop, I can feel the rainwater sloshing in my boots. The poncho has kept the bulk of me dry, but it's curtains for these socks. I'll have to see if I have a spare pair under my table.

At least inside, it's warm and dry, the heater providing a white-noise hum through the vents on the ceiling and the ever-present scent of cinnamon wafting a cozy vibe across the room.

The Embroiderie is a craft store. It's also a Craft store. We heard you liked crafts, so we got crafts for your Crafts so you can Craft while you craft. It specializes in all things stringy, glittery, and gluey for all your magical mess-making needs. Spell books line the back wall—except for the section blocked off by my mystical curtain—and every other square inch is filled with tables and shelves stuffed with both unburnable and extra burnable paper, pens that are always the color you need them to be, and yarn that never knots where you don't want it to, for all the *knotty magic* folk. The till, inside the door to the left, has a tapestry-sized cross-stitch hanging over it that Miss Tess made herself. It was basically her magical PhD project, stitching a handful of spells into and over each other to form what she now calls The Okay Conjunction after some kids' movie from the '80s.

I wanted to keep my job, so when she explained what it did—wards the shop against thievery, bribery, and general bad vibes—I wisely did not tell her I thought it reminded me of a topographical map of an oil-slicked swampland. Even if I'm not fond of how it looks, I can feel the calming vibes coming off it in waves as I shake off my poncho and step, squelch by squelch, farther into the store.

"Gemma," she calls, and I turn a full three-sixty, trying to catch a glimpse of her. I don't, so she must be behind one of the taller shelves toward the back. On my way there, I knock into a table full of crystals and immediately jump away. Some of those fuckers *burn* if they're in a bad mood.

Like a ghost passing right through a wall, Miss Tess appears without bumping into a damn thing. She's on the floor scooping up the toppled rocks before I can even utter, "Sorry," and the table display is back in place a moment later.

She stands, puts her hands on her hips, and smiles at a job well done. Her massive red curls bounce back into place, and the patterns on her long skirt shimmer. My boss has almost the exact vibe of an excited Miss Frizzle—if Miss Frizzle was desperately in love with shiny, messy magics instead of accessible sciences.

Then she turns to me, and the smile drops faster than the crystals. "Gemma."

It sounds so final, I almost turn and walk right back out into the rain.

But I don't. I need this job.

"Yes, Miss Tess?"

The rhyme makes her smile again, though this does nothing to dispel the feel of doom and gloom hanging over me. Her next words hammer the feeling home. "I have bad news."

She pauses, presumably for dramatic effect, the long lights along the ceiling shining in her round glasses.

"I need to move your table again."

"What? Where?" I demand before I can think better of it. Miss Tess, bless her, hardly blinks, but she does frown. I hold my hands up in supplication. "Sorry, sorry, just . . . Literally, where else could it go?"

I glance over at my curtain, which flutters lightly in the breeze from the heater. I'm already basically pressed against the wall back there. How much farther back could I possibly get?

As if she's read my thoughts, Miss Tess adds, "If we could maybe angle you differently. I have another shelf I want to put in back there. There's this new tarot display I've been eyeing, and it would look *so good* set up next to you while you work!"

I cross my arms and feel one eyebrow shoot up. "Are you trying to put me out of work? Sell people their own cards so they can séance at home?"

She scoffs, waving both hands in the air to clear the accusation like smoke. "You know half of them are buying because they're pretty, not because they're going to use them. And none of them can 'séance at home.' They don't have the"—she wiggles her fingers at me—"ghostly touch."

I resist the urge to wiggle my fingers back sarcastically.

But we both know I lost this argument long before I walked through the door. Miss Tess runs the store as a benevolent goddess and organizes it as if she's playing a game of

Tetris. I look sadly at my little space, a square only a few feet on each side—soon to be less—surrounded in a swath of dark velvet decorated with glittering stars hanging from a curved curtain rod. The stars don't hold any magic, but they help set the mood.

"It is a little darker in that corner, I guess," I concede. "If nothing else, it'll add to the—"

"If you say 'ambiance' one more time, I'm taking the curtain too."

I drop my face into my hands and groan. "You might as well fire me then!"

Miss Tess laughs, one hand grabbing onto my shoulder even as the other reaches to start rearranging another table. "You know I wouldn't let you go like that." As she lets go of my shoulder, her hand drifts to her hair, pushing it back and away from one ear.

I flinch as I catch a glimpse of my own handiwork. Miss Tess's left ear, shorn off and flat at the top, a little jagged where there used to be a piercing along the edge and now there's only half a hole.

The thing about my kind of magic is that it really does depend *a lot* on the ambiance. I'm just a medium, what some would call a "pseudo-necromancer" since I don't mess with the bodies. I see, hear, talk to, and translate for ghosts. And 99% of the time, none of that is the least bit tangible to a regular person. They'll get vibes and chills, and I've seen a few people puke at the shift in air pressure that comes with really strong ghosts, but nothing really physical. Nothing actually harmful.

So when I lashed out after a particularly shitty client accused me of being a fake, I didn't expect the lash to be so literal. I didn't expect it to actually hit Miss Tess, scratching up the side of her face and slicing the top of her ear clean off.

I didn't mean to hurt her. But that doesn't negate the fact that I did.

The skin on Miss Tess's ear has healed over, and she's stopped touching it quite so much like an anomaly she can't ignore, but her curly hair refuses to stay where she wants it on that side anymore. I hate that I notice it so much. I hate that she *makes* me notice.

I hate that I did it in the first place.

"I'll get everything squeezed back there, I promise," I assure her and start shuffling my way between displays before she can say anything else, careful not to knock any more tables over. As I reach for the curtain to pull it open, a shadowy hand darts out as if to slap me away, and I freeze.

The hand waves once through the air, then disappears.

I reach forward again, slower this time, and still feel the urge to jump away when I touch the fabric even though the shadow limb does not reappear. I hold my hand there for several seconds before pulling the curtain open.

Nothing.

But I know it's there. That fucking shadow.

For some reason, I thought it wouldn't be able to get me in here. It's shown up around the shop before, peeking through the windows and looming behind the shelves, but never in my séance space. Never behind the curtain. The stars on the fabric aren't magic, but necromancy tends to spook even the heartiest of magical beings at least a little. So if a shadow creature was going to be afraid of anything, it would probably be necromancy, right?

The bell over the shop's door rings, and I realize I'm still standing with the curtain thrown wide open. I'm ruining the whole spooky persona already! With one final scan of my tiny space, I step inside and pull the curtain closed behind me.

There's a light not quite directly over the space that shines in just enough that I can see my way around to get set up. I settle into one of the three chairs around the table, shifting the heavy wooden frame back and forth a few inches to test how much closer to the wall I can get without being entirely crushed. Not very, but it'll have to be enough.

I set my bag on the tablecloth hanging over my round table—soft, thin fabric depicting a series of golden eyes on a muddy red background—and start rummaging through it. The bag is perhaps the least ambiance-inducing item here. It's a gym bag I've had since high school, once bright blue and now something closer to a dusty navy, with several holes in the sides and one of the two straps only a few threads short of coming loose. I've been meaning to fix it, but my favorite needle and thread went missing recently, and I haven't had the bandwidth to go searching for them.

Inside the bag is everything I need to set the mood: the sweet-smelling incense to create a pleasant haze; a lacy maroon headscarf to pull back most of my hair while leaving my bangs to hang ominously over my eyes; a crystal ball because that's what people expect to see, and I aim to please; and finally, my tarot card deck.

I've had more than one over the years, but this one is my favorite. The art is abstract, geometric in some places and foggy in others, so you almost have to be looking at them from an angle to pick out the symbols, like one of those cereal box optical illusions. The edges of the cards have been worn soft from shuffling, and I've handled them so many times that I can identify which cards I've pulled from the feel of the fraying and the scratches and dents across the mazelike pattern on the back.

I can also tell with a shuffle if a card is missing. Today, it's not just one but two that have flown the deck. I dig through the bag several times before it becomes clear they're not there.

I flip through the deck quickly to take stock. I'm missing one major and one minor arcana—The Moon and the Four of Swords. Pesky bastards.

Shit. I don't have another deck with me, and I'm not buying a new set from Miss Tess. I would have to explain why, and how I lost cards out of a deck that I use almost every day. They're probably between the couch cushions, and wouldn't that just be a winning explanation from her failure of an employee? No, my customers will have to do without.

I'm lighting the incense when my curtain is pulled back. Time for my first session of the day.

I aim for smoky and mysterious when I look up and say, "Welcome, welcome! Sit and let your soul be—"

The shadow creature stands haloed by the fluorescent lights, its star-bright eyes shining, glaring down at me, and I freeze in place, nowhere to run, not even room to shove my chair back and bolt.

"Are you all right, dear?" The woman pulls her glasses off the top of her head and steps closer, revealing that she is solid and alive and not a curse. Well, not any more than any other customer is, at least. She smirks, and I know exactly what she's going to say before she says it. "You look like you've just seen a—"

"Not yet!" I say, with a loud laugh to cut her off.

She nods and turns back to hold the curtain open for someone else, while I breathe deep and implore my heart to stop pounding. A kid steps forward, a boy who must have recently reached the status of tween, his lanky form covered in clothes that all look at least a size too big for him. A battered-looking gray handheld gaming console is clutched in both his hands, closed and seemingly powered off. The game slot in the back is empty.

"Come on in, sweetie, and tell her what you wanted to say," the woman says, ushering him in.

The kid sits in one of the chairs while the woman closes the curtain before plopping down next to him. He fidgets with the handheld for a minute, his eyes following the twisting pattern of eyes on the tablecloth. Then he takes a deep breath and says, "My name is Sean, and I . . . want to talk to my mom."

I steeple my fingers thoughtfully and look at the woman next to him. I assumed this woman was his mother, but upon further inspection, it's clear they're family but not that close. They have similar eyes and hair, dusty blue and dusty blond respectively, but her chin's a little wider, his nose a little longer. Family features, but not the same ones. An aunt, maybe.

I look back to Sean and wait for him to meet my eyes, all spooky pretenses gone. This isn't a client looking for a show. This is a real person looking for a moment of peace. Maybe closure.

I get way too many of the former, especially during tourist season, the people at whom my emphasis on ambiance is usually aimed. They're here for the smoke and mirrors, ready to be dazzled and spooked. But occasionally, I'll get someone real, someone who has not come to gawk at the backwater medium in the tiny town on the way to a bigger destination. Someone like Sean, who's lost in more ways than one.

"What's that you've got there?" I ask softly, nodding at his hands.

He lifts the handheld console onto the table, resting both hands on top of it, as if he's scared it'll get up and run off. "It was my mom's. She always had it in her purse, so I could play while we were out on errands. But she left it at home when . . ."

I nod slowly and bring my hands carefully onto the table. "Clearly it was very special to her. That'll be a big help." I slide my hands forward a bit, and he flinches. "You can keep it right there if you want, I won't move it. I just need to touch it for a minute. Is that okay?"

Sean's lip wobbles for a second before he nods and lets his hands drop.

True to my word, I don't move the console an inch as I set one hand flat on top of it and close my eyes.

Oh. Yeah, the bond here is super strong. Some items I've been brought have had such little significance to their previous owner that making a connection is like trying to make out the words to a song in another language echoing down a long hallway. This is like hearing the song played in the room next door—muffled, as all connections are by the Veil of death, but mostly coherent.

I clear my throat softly and begin whispering the spell to open the Veil, the words of pressing, unlocking, and rejoining whistling through my teeth. My breath goes cold, and I'm so close to Sean, I see him shiver as I exhale. Mentally, I reach out along the line of magic drawing from the game console to the nearly invisible wrinkle in the world, the slight shimmer of the Veil, and push through into the darkness.

It's a darkness I know well. I was there myself last night.

But this time, when I open my eyes, it's not menacing shadows I see.

It's the misty figure of a woman whose features, though slightly blurred, are reflected in her son's face. She's got one hand on the back of his chair, the other resting on top of mine, still covering the game console.

I smile and look back at Sean, whose face is drawn in worry. "She looks just like you."

The woman next to him covers her mouth as Sean bursts into tears. "Is she here for real?" he asks between sniffles.

"For real, promise." I look up at the specter of his mom, who's leaning over him now. It's obvious she wants to hug him. "Ma'am, can you hear me?" Sometimes they can't—or won't—interact with anyone or anything other than the anchor temporarily holding them on this side of the Veil. But luckily, Sean's mom isn't like that, and she looks over at me curiously.

"What's she saying?" Sean asks, head swiveling around and tragically passing right through his mom's stomach.

"Nothing yet. Is there anything you want to say to her?"

His lip wobbles, and he reaches toward the woman who brought him in. She gives his hand a squeeze, and his mom incorporeally does the same to his other hand.

"Just that I love her and miss her a lot." His voice breaks a little on the last few words, but he powers through to finish with, "I wish she'd come home."

I look back up to the ghost, who is mouthing something, but there's no sound. *Shoot.* "Hold on a tick," I say, then whisper a few words of strengthening and twirl my pointer finger in a clockwise circle, like I'm turning up the volume on an old radio dial. Her words start to solidify, sort of skipping past my ears and buzzing directly into my brain.

"*—can't come home, I don't fit anymore, but you're safe with Aunt Rose. She loves you. I love you so, so much. You know that.*" The ghost fixes me with a desperate stare. "*He knows that, right?*"

"She wants you to know that she loves you so, so much," I say.

Before Sean can speak again, the woman next to him scoffs quietly, drawing the attention of both Sean's mom and me.

"Are you Aunt Rose?" I ask, and her face goes pale. *Aha.* She thought I was fibbing. The ghost raises one semi-transparent eyebrow, and her voice starts buzzing in my head again. "She says you'd better be taking care of Sean and not making him eat that—well, I'm not going to repeat the curse word for obvious reasons"—I wink at Sean—"but she says you'd better not be feeding him your tuna mac and cheese casserole."

This gets a fake gag and a laugh out of Sean. Rose bites her lip and crosses her arms but doesn't seem to have anything to say to that.

"Can I talk to her too?" Sean asks, settling a little more comfortably in the chair. His mom's hand passes over his head as she tries to brush the hair back from his face.

"You won't be able to hear her, but you can tell her anything you want, and I'll let you know what she says back."

He seems to think for a moment before asking, "Can I tell her about school?"

"*Of course you can, I want to hear everything. How are your teachers this year? Have you made any new friends? What's your favorite—*"

"Hold on!" I say to both of them. Careful to keep my left hand on the game console to hold the connection in place, I reach my right over to where the incense is still burning. I pluck the stick out of its holder and wave it briefly over Sean and through his mother. She's not solid enough to move his hair, but the lavender-scented smoke rises a little slower when it hits her. She watches this happen passively, unbothered by her own weak bodily presence. Weak, but not too weak to stick around a while.

"Okay," I say, quickly replacing the incense. "Ask away, you two. We've got all the time in the world."

Three

All the time in the world ends up being about two and a half hours before Sean's mom finally starts fading. I have to tell them to say goodbye, then I whisper the words of release that slice across my tongue like tiny razors and cut the ghost's tether to this side. She goes without complaint, and Sean, though still crying, is at least smiling a little on his way out.

As Sean meanders back and forth through sparkling displays on his way to the front of the store, Rose pulls me aside.

"Thank you," she says, and I realize belatedly that she didn't say a word the whole time. That was Sean's mom, but she was also Rose's sister. She takes one of my hands in both of hers, soft warm palms and thin cold fingertips, and squeezes. "He never got to ... She was going to the store, and there was a crash, and ..."

I set my free hand on top of hers. "I'm glad he got to say it this time."

She nods and lets me go. As she turns toward the

counter, I hear her mutter, "I can't believe she's still mad about that casserole. That was *one time*!"

Days where I really get to use my Craft are amazing, encouraging, and all too rare. The stark reality of my situation is that I'm not the only medium around. We're barely an hour out of a big city with plenty of more professional, and infinitely flashier, necromancers of all kinds, and the people who are willing to pay up will go there instead, even in the off season.

Miss Tess is pleased as punch though, all smiles as she offers them tissues on their way out.

When they're gone, she turns to me and beams. "Well, I think you've earned your keep for the day!"

Ah, yes, there it is. The weight of expectation. It drops back onto my shoulders like a backpack full of books.

Miss Tess doesn't seem to notice as she *pings* open the till and slips their money inside. I'll get a bit of it as a commission with my paycheck later this month. I should be looking forward to that little extra, but all I can think about is how many more paychecks I'll be worth. Will I make it to the spring, when the tourists start streaming back in? Do I even want to?

Yes. No. I need a drink.

"Coffee?" asks Miss Tess.

"What?" I demand, worried I've been speaking my bummer thoughts out loud.

"I said, you look cooked, do you need some coffee? I'm buying." She waves around her loyalty card for the nearest coffee shop, and the smell of beans seems to waft toward me from the little plastic rectangle.

"Sure," I say, trying not to sound too desperate as I hold

my hand out for the card. I can suddenly feel every minute between me and my bed.

Without warning, Miss Tess grabs my hand in both of hers, the card sandwiched tightly between our palms. "That obviously took a lot out of you. Why don't you go ahead and take your break too? Head on back with a latte for me when you're done, okay?"

I try to shrug it off, but she's not having it, ushering me out the door with assurances that she'll get anyone looking for my services on the schedule for later today.

Out on the sidewalk, it takes me several minutes to remember how to move. I hate that Miss Tess can see how tired I am. And not just because of last night's . . . *excursion*. My Craft doesn't always take so much out of me, only ever as much as I put into it, but I wanted to give Sean and his mom as much time as possible. However, even an hour of really reaching beyond the Veil is much more taxing than, say, an hour of playacting the fortuneteller stereotype. The latter is a whole different kind of work, tiring and soul-sapping in a more metaphorical way.

For a moment, I flash back to my hands in Miss Tess's, the pressure she put on them, then on me to leave. Was she trying to get rid of me? What could she need to do in there without me?

And—oh no—there it is again. The shadow in the window, wavering like a reflection on water, and I wonder . . . Has Miss Tess cursed me?

Why else would the thing not be constantly bothering me while I'm behind my dark little curtain in the shop? After all, she wouldn't send anything after me that would keep me from working. That's *her money* I'm making.

And after what I did . . . I can't argue with her motive.

See, there's a limit to what a medium should be able to do. Some stronger necromancers are more what non-magic people imagine: calling bones and bodies back to life for a short period of time, walking shamblers with enough locomotion to make it across a room, maybe lift a few heavy objects before falling apart. Others can do what I can with spirits but in a more tangible way, manifesting not just hazes and voices but whole beings that can be seen and felt, ectoplasmic void made whole.

I've never been able to do that stuff. Except the one time I didn't mean to.

It makes my stomach churn to think about now, and I glance up and down the street, fully expecting my tagalong specter to appear outside the shop, a threat as much as a reminder.

Yet, the only people on the street are the usual late-morning shoppers, shifting their tote bags from one shoulder to the other as they speed-walk by. I breathe.

I don't really want to think about Miss Tess cursing me.

But someone must have.

I feel myself wobble a little on my feet, and that's the push I need to make my way down the road toward the coffee shop. From outside the Embroiderie, I can just about see the sign, one of those old-fashioned wooden ones that's hung straight out over the doorway. It creaks with the breeze as I trot across the street and up to the door.

"Oh, shi—sorry!" I barely stop myself from cursing as the door swings open in my face, and Alan Cartwright, the oldest man I've ever seen this side of the Veil, comes trundling out, a coffee in one hand and his cane in the other.

He side-eyes me as he shoulders the door open wider.

"Impolite for a young lady to swear," he says by way of greeting.

"Sorry," I say again. "Long morning."

He looks me up and down with a frown. "Seems like it. The bags under your eyes say it all." *Gee, thanks,* I think, watching his jowls wag with every word. If I didn't know him, I'd think he had one foot in the grave already. But since I do know him, I believe it's going to require something stronger than death to take him down. "Is my appointment for next week still set?"

"Of course it is, Mr. Cartwright." As it has been every thirteenth of every month for the last two years. Thank goodness it wasn't today—I don't think I'd survive almost cussing in front of him *and* not having a full deck to do his hour-long reading with.

But I wasn't supposed to survive at all.

I wonder what he'd do if I didn't come back. Probably complain to Miss Tess. Maybe via formal, typewritten letter.

He nods once, deathly serious. "Well, get inside and get yourself some liquid energy. Better hurry before they run out of *eco-friendly* paper and plastic," he practically spits, waving the coffee cup in his hand for emphasis. Then he lifts it toward the creaking wooden sign and adds, "They might as well replace that one too, before some yuppie complains."

I glance up at the sign fondly. It's in the shape of a steaming ceramic mug, even though all the shop's drinks are served in compostable cardboard these days—much to Mr. Cartwright's chagrin. The mug is decorated with little black paw prints painted in a trail from bottom to top. The sign doesn't have the shop's name on it—even their loyalty card only has a picture of the mug and the member's name and number—but it's locally known as Aw, Beans.

"Have a good day, Mr. Cartwright," I say as I slide past him.

"You're welcome for the door," he replies before letting it slam closed with a rattle of its large metal bell.

I walk into the living definition of chaos.

The place is hoppin' with the late morning crowd, and I'm immediately assaulted by the sounds of several conversations, all being had at a volume a touch above "inside voices" so as to be heard over the intermittent whir of coffee beans being freshly ground. The smell competes with the miasma of sickly-sweet syrups wafting from the back wall where the numerous bottles are displayed like mismatched holiday ornaments. The owner, Mrs. Evelyn Brigsby, clad in a coat much too fluffy for any time other than deep winter and sunglasses much too thick for the gloomy day outside, sits at her usual table in the corner. It doesn't matter what the sky is doing; she wears sunglasses because she thinks it makes it impossible for people to see where she's looking. As if she's ever *not* staring down her baristas, silently willing them to upsell her latest concoction.

Evelyn enjoys imagining that she's the owner of a major franchise location that would surpass the likes of every name-brand coffee shop in the nearest city if she could only pin down the one drink recipe to end all drink recipes. Over the last few years, her drive has resulted in some of the most bitter, sugary, and upsettingly thick drinks I've ever had the displeasure of putting in my mouth.

But I always do. In solidarity with Aaron, Beans's longest-standing barista and my oldest and best friend.

Aaron is, in fact, behind the counter upselling to the ten-person-deep line of customers like his life depends on it.

Which it does, sort of, in the "need money to live" kind of way.

A flash of dusty gold hair from under his deep-blue cap, and he's jumped from the front counter to the back wall, which is covered in an assortment of coffee machines, tea steepers, steaming pitchers, scales, and shot glasses.

When I'm two customers away, Aaron catches my eye, turns distinctly away from the table where his boss is definitely *not* watching him, just ask her, and rolls his eyes to the ceiling. Sometimes I wish Aaron could read my mind, but since he has no magic of his own, we're forced to stick to our usual silent conversation tactics.

I raise an eyebrow as he rings up the front customer's order. *That kind of day, huh?*

He hands the customer their change, meets my gaze, and flattens his mouth. *You have no idea.*

My eyes dart from Aaron to Evelyn and back several times. *On a roll today, is she?*

The slightest nod as he wipes a few drops of melted whip from the counter. *And watching like a hawk.*

I nod solemnly in return. *Godspeed, friend.*

"Miss Gemma, how are you today?" he says in the cheerful customer service voice that makes me want to hit him. I know it's not really him behind that saccharine tone, but the condescension is so well-practiced, it hits home anyway.

"Stellar, Aaron," I say, my own voice not nearly as chipper. "I'm here for the usual for Miss Tess."

"Aw, and nothing for yourself? Let me talk you out of that." Winning smile. Lightning-fast glance toward Evelyn. Her sunglasses flash.

I bring a hand to my mouth thoughtfully. "I don't know . . . Have you got anything new and exciting on the menu?"

He leans back and takes a deep breath. "Our Wish It Was Winter latte will put you in mind of every pre-Christmas blowout you've ever had, with three shots of apple syrup, two shots of pumpkin syrup, one shot of cinnamon syrup, actual cinnamon, cardamon, and clove whipped into the milk, layered over a shot of espresso and drizzled with caramel over ice." By the time he's done speaking, he's out of breath and I can practically feel my teeth rotting out of my head. But I smile anyway, leaning onto the counter as if I'm truly intrigued instead of vaguely horrified.

"Sold! Give me one of those and a dirty chai latte, please."

"On it!" He gives me a thumbs-up before darting to the back counter.

I turn and look casually in the general direction of Evelyn. She's adjusting her sunglasses so she can speed-type something into her phone. She's smiling, so I hope it's something good for Aaron. He works way too hard for this place. She ought to pay him like she knows it.

Aaron reappears behind the register a moment later, two disposable cups in hand, one steaming and the other overflowing with the cinnamon-dusted whipped cream he's crammed in under the lid.

For a moment, Evelyn turns away fully, leaning over her phone like she's trying to read something secret, and Aaron takes the opportunity for a millisecond of freedom.

Sliding the drinks across the counter, he leans in and whispers, "Hey, still good for movie night this week?"

Oh shit, I almost forgot. After four years of semi-regular monthly meetups to trash on the best (read: worst) horror and/or chick flick we can find, it should have stuck in my head.

Aaron jerks away from the counter as a slender shadow slides across the polished laminate. A chill runs up my spine as it spills past the cups, bringing to mind the tarry smell of old gasoline which, for just a second, overpowers the smell of over-sweetened coffee.

The second is long enough to break my "world's best customer" façade, and I smack my hand onto the laminate with a *whack* that seems to blast through the room and vibrate up my arm. I feel a zing, like I've touched a live wire with wet hands, and then the shadow is gone, though my skin continues to tingle.

Aaron is holding one of his hands in the other, rubbing it carefully and looking back and forth across the counter. I hope he saw it, proof at last that I'm not crazy—but, no, he's not that flavor of concerned as he squats down to pull a towel from a cabinet below, frowning but not really afraid. He probably thinks I spotted a bug or something.

"Aaron!" Evelyn's honey-sweet voice calls from the side counter as she raises her sunglasses to sit on top of her perfectly coifed blond bangs. "Everything okay?" Her rose-red-lipsticked purse turns into a comical frown, but her dark eyes dart from me to Aaron, then once around the barista station before landing back on me. I know in my bones if she had even an ounce of magic to her name, her gaze would kill.

Aaron pops back up over the counter, appeasing smile plastered across his cheeks and one hand wrapped in the towel. "Yes, ma'am! Gemma was just saying she *has to*"—he smacks the counter with his non-toweled hand with all the gusto of a salesman talking up a car—"try your latest and greatest! Right, Gemma?"

Evelyn's gaze never leaves my face.

The shadow is gone, and I'm holding up the line now.

I plaster on the biggest, fakest smile I can muster. "You bet! And thanks, I'm *so* excited to try this!" I hold up the metric ton of sugar squeezed into a large-size cup.

This seems to appease Evelyn for the time being. Her pout bounces back into a smile, and she makes a show of dropping her glasses back over her eyes before slinking back to her table.

I release the breath I've been holding the moment her eyes aren't directly on me anymore and turn back to Aaron. "Are you okay?" I whisper, frowning down at his hand.

Aaron, seemingly assured that Evelyn is not about to end his entire career, recovers as well. "Yeah, no worries. Must have spilled something here earlier, I think I burned myself." He readjusts the towel, and I see red, angry-looking skin on the side of his hand poke through before he covers it up. "Oh, you still need Miss Tess's drink!"

"I'll come back for it. I have another stop to make." I wave my free hand at him, resisting the urge to apologize. Aaron didn't spill a damn thing to cause that burn. I reach into my pocket to retrieve my own cash to pay. I don't need Miss Tess's charity for my own drinks.

"I'll bet you do," Aaron mumbles as he rings up the order, and I feel the words hit me right in the gut.

What is that supposed to mean?

Is he . . . upset with me? Did I freak him out with my freak-out? He's still smiling, but he's not meeting my eyes. Instead, he's glancing around the floor, probably looking for whatever he thinks he spilled, whatever caused that burn.

He hands me back my change, and I'm too busy trying to figure out if he put it in my hand harder than usual to think about how much it is. I drop it all into the tip jar next to the till, grab my drink, and hurry out the door.

Outside, the sun is trying very hard to shine through the clouds. It's almost bright enough to hurt my eyes, but not bright enough to actually see the shape of the sun through the haze.

It's plenty bright enough to see the notes scribbled on the sides of the cups though. On my chai, in thick, dark marker, Aaron wrote BRING POPCORN. I chance a look inside, but Aaron is back in full swing, clearly going in for another upsell.

Of course I'm going to bring popcorn. It's his turn to pick the movie, so it's my turn to bring the snacks. I knew that. Or, I would have remembered eventually. And he knows that . . . right?

I turn the other cup to read it, careful not to tip it too far and send sugary foam sliding out of the hole in the top.

The side of this cup just says CALLIE.

I did not spend my hard-earned money for a coffee call-out post about the girl I've had a crush on since high school. I think about tossing the cup in the trash can outside the shop if only to prove that's not who I was thinking of when Aaron described the drink to me. But he's my best friend. He knew. And that *was* who I was thinking of.

I suppose I deserve it. I really could have gotten him in trouble with that fucking shadow. If it knocked anything over while Aaron was behind the counter, or worse, if it busted one of the machines constantly percolating piping-hot coffee and he got hurt . . .

No. Nobody got hurt. The drink is already paid for. It would be a shame to waste the calories.

Right. To the library it is, then.

Four

Without tourists to entertain and be entertained by, the library becomes the central hub for both studying and socializing. There are events almost every evening through fall and into winter, weather permitting, from craft nights to movie showings to read-alongs to wine nights—which somehow tend to bleed into the other happenings regardless of what the theme of the night was actually meant to be.

Later this evening, the staff will give up the pretense and have a wine and paint night. As I push open the doors, I can already smell the bitter scent of well-used watercolors being set out. The tables in the back room, the round kind right out of a school cafeteria, are covered in long sheets of paper and peppered with brushes, water cups, and plastic pallets already splattered with muddy rainbows of color from previous events.

Nancy, the head librarian, walks with quick, tiny steps from place setting to place setting, readjusting the supplies and dropping off crinkled coloring books. Her messy brown bun flops side to side as she shifts the chairs around the tables, counting and recounting as if she's not sure they have enough.

I open my mouth to greet her, but before I get a single word out, she's already turned to me and is pointing to the stacks on the other end of the building. "She's back there." Then she's gone again.

I bite my tongue, embarrassed. Is it that obvious why I came by? Was it something on my face? Is it the drink? Can she smell the syrup from here? I consider following her, offering to help with the setup for this evening to pretend I'm not here to see someone specific. But she already knows and already called me on it, so that would be even more embarrassing.

Ugh. She must think I'm awful. I slink away in the direction she'd indicated before she comes back and I burst into flames.

On the way back to the stacks, I spot Henry, the former head librarian, wandering between the shelves. Tall and blocky, he always looks like he ought to be coaching a football game, not organizing a cart of books. Maybe that would have saved him—he passed four or five years ago from a heart attack. Callie likes to tell people he died here in the library to see them freak out, but that's not true; he just left his soul here on his way out.

I mutter a spell, the same one I used to open the Veil for Sean's mom, gesturing toward him with one of my coffee-laden hands in a "come here" motion.

He pauses for half a second, then continues his semi-transparent stroll through—literally through—another row of shelves.

"Damn," I say. I'm going to have to come up with something stronger. I've been trying to get Henry through the Veil, where he belongs, every few months since he died, but nothing so far has even been able to hold his attention. I shrug and continue on my way. As long as he's not going full poltergeist and throwing books around—which I doubt he'd ever do, even in death—I guess he can hang out a little longer.

The "stacks" of our library are a little more literal than I think they're supposed to be. But since the town's collection runs mostly on donations, the books really do show up in piles upon piles, and they rest in those piles until Apprentice Librarian Calliope Tynes finds them their foster homes on the shelves.

The room where the stacks are kept was once a class-room, where the library's events were held until about ten years ago when they got the funding to expand the building. They did not, however, spend a penny of the new room's budget to fix up the old room, so its dingey white-and-brown linoleum floors and stained tan walls reflect every heated book club meeting and school-age craft class it ever hosted.

I knock with the hand holding my drink before slipping into the room, and a mop of messy black hair shoots into view.

Unlike my own dingey locks, Callie's hair has never not looked silky and clean, impressively holding shapes it somehow seems to achieve in spite of gravity. It shines in the sun like obsidian, even catching the spare light coming in through the window. I think if I could run my hands through it just once, it would fix me. Not in the "breaking my curse" kind of way, but in the "I'd never want for anything ever again" kind of way.

Okay, that's not true. I'd still want to stare into her eyes, blue with the lightest fade into hazel at the edges, like she's got the whole wide world in her gaze. I'd still want to trace the pattern of freckles across her cheeks and over her nose. I'd still want to know what the purple-tinted gloss on her lips tastes like.

"Oh my god," she says, throwing both hands over her mouth in shock.

I turn, taking in the library behind us, looking for any signs of the shadow creature. It could be anywhere among the shelves. But nothing moves, so I turn back to Callie, worried it slipped past me and went for her, but—

When I turn, she's right in front of me, and I freeze.

My heart rate drops back to a normal level when I realize she's smiling, her hands clasped excitedly, and her eyes glued to my hands.

"Oh my god," she repeats, "did you bring me coffee? How did you know?"

"Uh . . . lucky guess?"

She laughs, and I'd buy every drop of coffee in Beans to make it happen again. "You're too funny! You couldn't have known our coffee maker bit the big one this morning. Unless . . ." She leans forward, squinting at me—the few inches I have on her mean she has to rise onto her toes to look me right in the eye. "Do coffee machines have ghosts? Did it tell you itself?"

It's my turn to laugh, startled-sounding and too loud, but Callie smiles anyway. "No, I have not yet met a coffee maker ghost. But the moment I do, you'll be the first to know. But, uh . . ." I readjust my grip and hold out the sugary brew. "This is for you. Evelyn's latest. Aaron made it sound pretty good though, so . . ."

"He always does." She takes the cup in both hands,

sniffing deeply. "Fuck yes, just what I needed. Well, maybe a little adjustment."

She looks directly down into the cup as if trying to see the whole drink through the inch-thick layer of whipped cream, and for a few seconds, her eyes take on a light pink glow.

Callie's Craft is, in my opinion, the most useful Craft in existence. I can talk to ghosts. Others can alter peoples' moods, mold matter into new shapes, or make the weather cooperate for the length of a wedding or a professional sports game. But you know what none of us can do any of that shit without? *Energy.* And Callie can infuse any drink she likes with exactly the kind of energy one needs. Physical, mental, emotional—you need a boost, put your drink of choice in her hand for a minute, and you've got it.

Callie herself, however, says her power is practically useless unless she's catering to desperate moms on the go. But the power to imbue a consumable drink with exactly the kind of energy a person needs to live through one more day is more than most people could hope for. If she and Aaron, with his barista skills, ever opened a shop of their own, they'd make a killing and both be able to move out of this tiny town, on to something bigger and better.

"Okay." She sighs after a good, long sip that leaves a smudge of whipped cream foam on her lip. I can't think of a clever way to point it out, and it's also unbearably cute, so I don't comment. "Your turn."

"What?" I look at the drink in her hand. "I'm not drinking that! It'll kill me!"

"Gem, you already kinda look like death warmed over," she says with a wry smile, holding out a hand. "Give me your drink."

Oh. Right. I hand over my dirty chai, and she gives it the same rosy-eyed treatment before handing it back. I swear it's warmer from her hands. "What did you put in there?" I ask.

She frowns, and I try not to find that cute too. Doesn't work. "Just a bit of physical *oomph* to go with the espresso. I hope that's what you're needing. You look *exhausted.* Is Tessica working you to the bone over there?"

"Ha." I wave off her concern. "Not at all, there's hardly enough work to keep me busy this time of year. I just . . . didn't sleep well last night."

"Again?"

She doesn't mean anything by it, I know that. But the mild accusation in the question hurts anyway.

"Are you sure you don't want to go see a doctor? You know my mom's got people in the city . . ."

I shrug, my usual answer to this very question. "You know I've never slept well. Why try to change that now?"

She lets out a resigned sigh and points to my cup. "Well, once that wears off, you should be good and tired. Make sure you're home at a reasonable time tonight so you don't crash on the way."

"Aye-aye, captain!" I say with a little salute, which is enough to bring a smile crawling back across her face. The lip gloss glints. "And, uh, thanks."

She raises her own cup in return. "No, thank *you.*"

Five

Back at home, the pleasant hum of the day quiets into something much less comfortable. I miss when I was little, when I felt safe at home, when I didn't know any better.

Once upon a time, the kitchen always smelled like mom's cooking—usually the earthy scent of paprika hanging over whatever else was on the menu that night. The air was warm with the constant movement of living bodies, and I could aways trust my parents to chase the shadows away with a laugh.

But now I constantly feel like I'm waiting for the other shoe to drop. Or for a reason to drop the shoe myself.

It's too quiet. I live alone now, but the house used to be home to our nuclear family of four and would play host to a whole parties' worth of relatives on holidays. Childhood friends used to grace these halls on the regular.

Now, I'm afraid to have anyone over.

I don't want them to get hurt. To have that *thing* burn

them with its touch or catch them in some catastrophe like my mirror-turned-shrapnel.

I move through the kitchen and into the living room and freeze as something dark and looming appears in the corner of my eye, in front of the living room window, behind the couch—

I'm staring for several seconds, holding my breath, waiting for it to pounce, before I realize that the thing is not moving, and several more seconds pass before I recognize it for what it really is: a pillow. The one I stuck behind my head while I sat there the other night trying to find a comfortable angle to wallow in.

No, wait. What was I actually doing? I had my laptop, and a bottle of soda, and my tarot cards . . .

My cards.

I lunge for the couch and tear all the pillows, cushions, and the crocheted blanket from my mother off the frame. I dig my hands into the gritty upholstery, pushing stale crumbs and forgotten coins out of the way, hoping to feel an edge of thick, printed cardstock somewhere in the darkness. But no luck. My hands come back dusty but otherwise empty.

I hold on to hope while doing a similar search of the space under the couch, in case my missing cards slid to the floor. If they're not here, if I didn't lose them in the shuffle this morning . . . How long have they been missing? I can't remember, and a wave of fatigue hits with the confirmation that my favorite deck will continue to be incomplete.

I can barely even imagine making it all the way up to my bed.

Callie wasn't kidding, I think as I force myself to my feet. Whatever she did to my drink earlier must have been way more potent than normal. None of her treatments have ever dropped me this hard before.

The house is not big. It was built in 1880 and updated enough over the years to keep our family comfortable. At least until my parents decided it wasn't anymore. Or maybe it was too much work. Either way, they figured it was time to move out, and as the last child in the home, they offered it to me for a fraction of what they probably could have gotten by putting it up on the market. So now, at least on paper, the house is mine. It and its creaky stairs, stained walls, and definitely haunted closets.

I mean it. There's a kid in the closet of the smallest bedroom who just stands there, looking around like he's waiting for someone to find him—that I already have found him doesn't even register. I've seen a few spirits like that, who never made it across the Veil or maybe never even tried to, much like Henry in the library. I'd call it a shame, but the kid doesn't seem unhappy, and he's never bothered us. But the attic . . . even I don't go anywhere near the spirits up there. Which is for the best, because they have violently agreed that they do not want me around either.

As for the rest of the house, I want to say it's a work in progress, but that progress is so slow-going, I'm likely to still be working on it by the time I'm old enough to hand the house down myself. Like Sarah Winchester, my work will never be finished. Unlike Sarah Winchester, I like to think the house will make more sense when I'm done with it, not less.

Of course, that would require me to stop being afraid of every shadow, of which there are many.

I know the house isn't to blame for the curse. Not all the

calls that come from inside the house are nice, but none of them are curse-level malicious.

I realize I'm staring up the stairwell, feet weighed to the floor by the inevitability of the impeding climb.

I'm so tired.

I'm also tempted to drag myself back out into the woods. But what good would that do?

I drag myself step by step upstairs instead, only barely managing not to catch my foot on the crooked stair halfway up. *I'll get to it,* I tell myself for the umpteenth time. *It's on the list.* At the top of the stairs, my eyes snag on the fractured shine of my broken mirror in pieces on the bathroom floor. *Yeah, yeah, that too.*

It's the last coherent thought before I faceplant onto my bed and pass out cold.

Six

"Hey, stranger!" Mom says as she swings the door open for me, as if I'm not here at their little rancher home every other week.

"Long time, no see," I joke back. "I brought the milk!"

For once, the chilly rain was good for something: keeping my single grocery item cold on the way here. I offer Mom the plastic bag—seemed silly for one quart of milk, but there was no way to hold it *and* keep my bike upright—and her hand flickers toward it before flying away as she seemingly realizes the whole package is dripping wet.

"Bless you, hon, these potatoes were about to end up dryer than the backyard."

I laugh sarcastically, wiping my rain-soaked boots on the doormat. I close the door behind me and follow her through their small living room, past their small dining table, and into their massive, well-equipped, and oppressively clean kitchen.

"You can set that on the counter," Mom says, practically jogging across the room to grab a towel off the oven. She trots back and makes a show of wiping down the bag, the milk carton, and then the gray-and-white marble counter around it before finally deigning to take the milk to the large pot of mashed, but dry, potatoes.

"Need a hand with anything?" I ask, though I already know the answer will be—

"No, all set here, hon! Why don't you set the drinks out?" She gestures to three glasses already full of iced tea sitting on the opposite counter.

I take a glass in each hand and press the third against my chest with one arm, then head to the dining room. The dining table is old but stable. The only clear signs of wear are a few scratches that peek out from under the lacey blue place-mats, onto which I deposit our drinks. The dishes and cutlery are stacked on one end of the table, and I start setting them in front of our usual seats just in time for Dad to emerge from the hallway.

"Gemma!" he exclaims like he's surprised to see me. "Glad you could make it." He comes around the table to grab me in a bone-crushing hug, which I try to return with half as much enthusiasm. After he releases me, he claps me on the shoulder, then turns to the kitchen to help Mom bring in the food: a large plate carrying what looks to be several pounds of fried chicken breasts, so crispy, I can already feel my teeth crunching through the coating; a glazed ceramic bowl full to the brim with roasted brussels sprouts, glistening with oil and peppered with, well, pepper, and salt, and a "dash" of paprika I can smell from here; and of course, the mashed potatoes, now made creamy with the milk and bits of yellow butter melting into the fluffy white waves.

They set everything on the runner in the middle of the table, and Mom says, "Dig in!"

And dig in I do. I snag a piece of chicken, which lands

on my plate with a delightful clatter, and am scooping a second spoonful of potatoes next to it when the game begins.

"How have you been, hon?"

Ping.

"Not bad. Tired."

Pong.

"Oh, you'd better be taking care of yourself!"

Ping.

"I am. I bike everywhere, you know."

Pong.

Conversations with my family have two settings: ping-pong and dodgeball.

Dodgeball is more stressful, for me at least. It involves ducking under comments either aimed directly at me or in the general direction of something distasteful that I disagree with but can't bring myself to fight about. Maybe that makes me a coward, but I was never the type to argue with my parents, even when it probably would have done us all some good to get things out in the open. Nod and smile. *Sure, I agree. Where's the ketchup?*

Right now, though, we're in ping-pong territory, a less openly threatening but no less insidious game that can lull you into a false sense of security before snapping at you with the speed of a cat lunging for a chicken bone.

Speaking of which . . .

"How's work?" Mom asks, *pinging* directly into dangerous territory.

Dad's mouth is blessedly full, the crunching of fried chicken audible, as I answer.

"The usual. Miss Tess has got some new sales display going up soon, so I'll have to work around that." He's still chewing. Safer subject, go! "What about you guys, any new projects lately?"

Pong.

"You know your father, when he's not working on the house, he's working on the boat."

That one brings a smile to my face. "Still?" My parents have a cool old sailboat. It's important to note, however, that the boat has not seen water deeper than a backyard puddle for years. Decades, maybe. "Working on the boat" has never meant getting it functional enough for sailing or for sale. No, instead, Dad has been working for ages to make it into his own personal ground-level treehouse. It's acted in turns as a game room, a shed, a summer pool house, and on one occasion when some cousin or other was out of the country and needed her pets looked after, a chicken coop.

I'm about to ask if he's gotten all the scat out of the carpet when my mom's phone goes off. The familiar little jingle lets the whole table know it's Brett, my brother. She's gone before the first string of notes tapers off, politely taking the call in the living room.

Leaving me and Dad alone.

I must have had something in common with my dad once upon a time. I mean, we used to hang out. Is it called hanging out when you're a teen and it's your dad, or is that supposed to be called, like, *bonding*? Anyway, there was time spent in each other's company that I remember being fun and not stressful. Moments that did not make me feel like holding my breath, waiting for the next blow.

Now, though, I can practically feel the dodgeball whizzing through the air right at my face.

"So, how's school?"

POOMH.

He knows I haven't been to class in more than a year. I quit when the workload got to be too much, when it became more math than magic and my brain couldn't keep up. The magic is intuitive to me—it's the logic behind it, when someone tries to "make it all make sense," that I can't fathom. I've been tossing around the idea of taking night classes, one at a time, to finish my General Magic Studies degree, but by now I can't remember if I wanted to take the classes for myself or if that was a cover to keep the questions at bay.

If it was the latter, I suppose it hasn't worked.

"Haven't signed up for anything new yet. I'm still looking."

"Hmm." *Hmm. Eloquent.* "And the job is okay with that?"

As if Miss Tess cares if I have credentials as long as I'm doing my job. "Yep. Turns out I can still talk to the ghosts without a piece of paper saying I can."

I make a show of scooping the perfect bite onto my fork—steaming chicken under buttery potatoes with a lightly browned half-sprout on top—afraid if I look up and make eye contact, the ball I dodged will hit me on the rebound.

My dad sighs. "You used to be so excited about writing your own spells. What happened?"

POOMH. A second dodgeball hidden in the shadow of the first.

I think of the stack of notebooks in my bedroom closet, taking up a whole shelf by themselves, their spines decorated with gold and silver embellishments, leather imprinted with leaves and flowers, covers in all colors and edges metallic, sprayed in pastels, or pristine white. Some aren't even out of the plastic they came in. Some I bought myself in a fit of misplaced inspiration. Others were gifts, theoretically well-meaning but, in the end, useless.

Every time I pick one up, my stomach flips and my head spins. That's not magic. It's fear, plain and simple, of being judged and found wanting.

Fear of being seen in a way I never wanted to be. Again.

But instead of bringing up where those feelings come from, I shrug and chew my perfect bite. It's not a satisfactory answer for either of us, but we're both saved when Mom comes back and plops down in her chair.

"Brett says hi!" she chirps, and Dad smiles.

I used to want to make Dad smile like that.

"He says he'll be back to stay with us in a few weeks, won't that be nice?" She looks at me, and I flash a thumbs-up while taking a long sip of tea. "Gosh, we haven't seen him in almost a year. He's been so busy! We should call up Aunt Sue and Uncle George, they'll want to see him too. Oh, and Miss Tess, I'm sure she's missed him. Who else?"

"I think I'm sick that day," I mumble as I stab a brussels sprout and push it into my potatoes. When I lift it to my mouth, it leaves behind an oily indent.

"You don't mean that," Dad asserts with a frown, pointing his own chicken-laden fork at me. "You love your brother."

Of course I love my brother. But I don't love having to share him with a hundred other people at once. Brett always was the personable type; he knew everyone, and everyone knew him. He only ever made good impressions, even before his mood-altering magic kicked in. It seemed exhausting.

But he always made time for me, so there's that. "I'll come see him! On a different day, you know, when it's less crazy."

"You don't even know what day it's happening," he says.

I shrug. "Well, whatever day it is, I'm sick until everyone else leaves." I smile big and wide. He doesn't look pleased, but he doesn't push anymore.

"Now," says Mom, settling back into her chair and picking up her fork. "What did I miss?"

"Nothing exciting," I say. *Ping.*

"Good." She spears a half-charred brussels sprout. "How's the house?" *Pong.*

I grimace, but I hope it comes across as a smile. "Still standing!" *Ping.*

Through a mouthful of chicken, Dad adds, "Those closets still giving you grief? I could come up there and take the doors off, no problem."

"Dad, taking the doors off isn't going to make the ghosts any less restless. They'll just find something else to rattle."

He sighs. "You and your ghost stories."

POOMPH.

Dad lived in that house. Raised us in that house. Saw what I could do firsthand in that house. But to him, the ghosts were never real enough. Phantom breezes and violently shaking doors with no one behind them could only mean the house needed some fixing up. I'm sure half the weight of the place is caulk and spackle by now. He's wished plenty of times—out loud even, though in places I'm sure he thought I wouldn't hear—that I'd either gotten more useful magic, like Brett's, or no magic at all.

Neither of my parents have magic, which isn't entirely unusual. Sometimes it skips a generation or two in a family line, and it's no wonder two people who got skipped got together. But the way my dad talks, it's like there was never a whiff of magic in his family history at all, even though I know Great Aunt Kat could make a painting wink and change the color of her dress on a whim. I don't have lots of memories of her, since she died when I was four, but I do have those.

Mom, on the other hand, has never once said she thinks my magic is useless. But she doesn't dispute Dad about it either. In private, I was always welcome to tell her about the ghosts I was able to bring through the Veil, any spiritual happenings in and around the house, and she was the first person I told when I got the job with Miss Tess.

Even now, Mom just gives me a small smile and a roll of her eyes. *Dad, amirite?*

When I was a kid, and even as a teenager, I thought it was kind of fun, like Mom and I had a special thing only she and I could talk about. But the older I get, the more frustrating it is that she doesn't defend me. It's probably not a fight worth having, but it stings a little that she won't have it anyway.

"You know your dad is always happy to come help fix anything up!" Mom offers.

I pull a smile across my face as tight as a rubber band, and just as ready to snap. "I know." I do know.

Mom's looking at me like she expects me to say something else. Uh. Shit. What else can I say?

"Thanks!" I add. *Ping.*

Mom nods; that was all she needed. "Well," she says, shrugging off the conversation like a wet coat. "Who wants dessert?" *Pong.*

Mom rushes to the kitchen before I can answer and reappears seconds later with a plate displaying a batch of tiny, bite-sized cheesecakes. I take one with a smile and pop it into my mouth. The creamy, cold middle spills out from between the crumbly graham cracker base and the thin chocolate topping as I bite down. Did I say Mom didn't have magic? Every time she bakes, I rethink that statement.

When the cakes are gone and both parents are sitting back in their seats, sipping tea and humming contentedly, I stand and start collecting plates.

"Thanks, hon," Mom says, her eyes fluttering closed as the food coma sets in.

"No problem!" I stack all the plates, forks, and knives together and head into the kitchen.

The sink is empty, brushed steel shining in the light of the lamp hanging over the counter. I wonder how long I could stand here before they come looking for me. I'm only here at all because if neither me nor Brett come visit them at least a few times a month, they get cranky, and he's been too far away to take that bullet for ages.

I turn on the water. Steam fills the air around me as I grab a plate and start scrubbing.

Rain pounds on the window above the sink. A few stray leaves are plastered to the screen on the outside. Riding back is going to be hell. How long would I have to be here to wait the weather out?

In the dark reflection on the glass, a darker figure looms behind me. I startle, dropping the plate in my hand back into the sink and wincing as it crashes into the others.

"Gemma? You okay?"

"Fine, Mom!" *Don't come in here!* "Nothing broke!" I look down into the sink to make sure I didn't just lie, and lucky for me, all the dishes are indeed still in one piece. But when I reach over to turn off the water, I see a stream of blood dripping over my fingers.

I move my hand under the running water to rinse the blood away, but suddenly, the water is scalding hot, immediately tingeing my whole hand red, and I pull it back with a yelp. The water goes black, gushing out in steaming waves that look like acid. It's filling the sink, rising to the edge, and I don't want to reach over it to turn off the tap, afraid getting too close will burn my whole arm off. It reaches the lip of the sink and spills over—not like water but like thick, rolling smoke. The smoke seems to rise toward me before dissipating entirely.

The sink is empty of everything but soapy water and dishes. The water running from the tap is clear.

"Gemma?"

I practically jump out of my skin before turning to see my dad in the doorway, one hand on a hip, one eyebrow raised curiously.

"You okay?" he asks, looking pointedly at the sink. "Did you, uh, *see* something?"

A glance at the window confirms the shadow is still there, watching. I need to get Dad out of here before it starts in with the waterworks again. I shrug. "Nope, just turned the tap on a little too hot."

He rolls his eyes before heading back to the table.

I look down at my reddened hand and find a small cut on the side of one finger, still oozing red, but pulling each plate carefully out of the sink reveals no shards or edges I could have been nicked with. I turn the water off and let the sink drain, squinting to look for anything that might have been submerged, but there's nothing.

When I look back up to the window, the shadow is gone.

Five more minutes. And then I'll go home.

Seven

I'm still shaking the rainwater off my umbrella when Aaron opens his door. The moment he looks down at my hands, I know I've fucked up.

"Oh, uh . . ."

"You forgot, no worries." He steps aside to let me into his apartment.

I walk past him, wringing my hands as if that will magically conjure the snacks it was my responsibility to procure. I don't even know if there's magic that does that.

I can't believe I forgot. *Again.*

"I'm sorry, I totally meant to grab the popcorn before I came over. We can order out if you want, my treat!" I can't look at him while I make the offer, afraid of the disappointment I'll see in his eyes.

He shifts in front of me so I have no choice though, and to my relief, it's amusement I find instead. "I said no worries, I've got us covered!" As I kick off my shoes by the door, he heads to the kitchen and flings open a cabinet, revealing an extra-large box of movie theater butter popcorn. He pulls out a bag with a flourish, removes the plastic, and plops it into the microwave.

I should be thinking, *Thank goodness we won't have movie night without snacks!*

I should be thinking, *Aaron's a smart guy, I knew he'd come through.*

Instead, all I'm thinking is, *He knew I'd forget. He had that box because he knew I'd forget and was prepared for me to fail him again.*

My eyes fall to my shoes as I consider putting them back on and taking a non-sexual walk of shame home. But the thought of slipping my feet back into the damp sneakers makes me want to cry almost as much as disappointing my friend does.

Aaron drops onto his couch as the popcorn starts popping, the drone of the microwave and the smell of salty butter filling the space. He pulls open a drawer built into his coffee table to reveal a lineup of tightly packed DVD cases. Aaron might be the only person I know that's shirked streaming services entirely. He doesn't have cable, either. 100% of his video entertainment comes from YouTube and his collection of DVDs.

"What're we feeling today?" he asks as he peruses the titles. "I got the snacks, so you get to pick again." I know from experience the drawer is organized first by genre, then by color—it's easier for him to identify the case than to read the movie name, supposedly, though he claims that has nothing to do with what he calls his "raging dyslexia."

I hardly have a right to answer. Here I am, mooching off of his movies, his house, and his snacks. He should at least get to pick what we watch. To put off answering, I rush to the microwave as the popcorn scent starts inching from salty to burned and quickly pull the bag out.

"Uh," I start as I carry the bag over, pinching one of the top corners between two fingers so the steam can't reach me. "Horror?"

"Sick." He slides his hand to the right side of the drawer. After hemming and hawing for a few seconds, he digs a finger into the drawer to dislodge one of the plastic cases. "How about this?"

I nod without really looking at it. Whatever he wants is good. "Looks great!"

He jumps up off the couch as I sit down, and I watch as he carefully removes the disc from the case and slides it into the DVD player. I hold the bag of popcorn awkwardly in my lap until he comes back, then offer it to him to open himself. He does, ripping at the top, then leans the bag toward me— an offering. I take a few pieces and sit back as if that's all I'll need for the night. My stomach grumbles in protest, but I ignore it.

The movie turns out to be a slasher, all buckets of fake blood and practical skin-ripping effects. Aaron has a YouTube channel bookmarked for stuff like this, one creator who goes into the details behind the horror and all the cool —and dangerous—effects the actors get to deal with. I haven't seen the analysis of this one, but who needs YouTube when you've got Aaron?

"So this scene here," he starts without me asking, "was shot in *one day* because they could only rent the lot for a few hours at a time, and the lead actor there had to be strung up in a harness for, like, the whole day. And see that wound? That prosthetic was made by the same artist who did that fantasy movie we watched last month—shit, what was his name? You know the one!"

I nod even though I do not know the one. The details don't always stick with me, but I love hearing him get excited. As he expounds the intricacies behind the head we just saw explode into a mess of gore and goo, his enthusiasm calms me enough to take the last handful of popcorn without feeling like a dick.

When he stops talking, I assume he's gone back to watching the bloodbath in silence. Until I glance over and realize he's got his phone out and is tapping the screen quickly. It's angled away from me, so I can't see what he's doing. His forehead is scrunched up, and he's frowning.

"Everything okay?" I ask, hoping he'll assure me it's his mom asking for a copy of another old recipe. She sent him off on his own with the family recipe book in hopes that he'd add to it over the years, but so far, it's only resulted in her reaching out once or twice a week asking for a recipe she didn't think to copy down before he left.

His frown gets deeper for a second, and he leans the phone screen away from me even more, then seems to realize he's doing it and presses the button on the side to put the screen to sleep entirely. "All good, nothing to worry about. Hey, did you catch that? This director makes them practice those screams for him before he even lets them get in front of the camera, isn't that wild?"

The sound of his voice and the movie fade into the background, and the popcorn sours in my stomach.

I wonder if he was talking to . . .

Then of course he wouldn't want to tell me, wouldn't want me to see. I'm the reason they broke up.

For a second there, he looked almost . . . hostile. Not just as if he didn't want me to see but that I am not *allowed* to see.

We used to tell each other everything. I was his first friend when he moved here—mostly his doing, being that he's the second most social person I've ever met, right after Brett. They'd have gotten along if Brett hadn't left by the time Aaron settled in. I think about that sometimes too: how we're only friends by chance, that he could have easily been here with Brett, telling Brett all about his favorite movies and sharing all his secrets. Brett wouldn't have forgotten the popcorn.

My eyes glaze over as I stare at the TV, the running characters becoming blurred blobs in my vision.

Does Aaron even want me here? He's clearly got someone else he could excitedly tell all his favorite film facts to. When did they get back together? How long ago? It's been a whole year since the breakup, since I made that *stupid* comment to Aaron and pulled them apart for my own selfish reasons. God, why am I such a . . .

I glance at Aaron, looking for a hint of what's actually going on, any indication at all that I'm more than a warm body to keep him company.

As I watch, the shadow creature rises slowly over the arm of the couch, directly behind Aaron.

I scream and kick one leg straight out before I can think, and my foot crashes through the now empty bag of popcorn and swings up into Aaron's chin, sending his head flying back with a crack of teeth.

"Shit, what—" he demands, leaning forward and covering his face with his hands. I feel bad, but at least he's out of the way. The shadow moves around the couch as if to sneak up on us from behind. I jump up, banging my shin on the coffee table. It's right there. *It's so close!*

"What the fuck do you want from me?" I shout as I fling myself around the other end of the couch. I try to think of a spell for dispelling, anything I can call on without extra components. My fingers twitch the shapes of runes as I crawl across the thin carpet, coming to rest on my knees with a clear view of—

Nothing. There's nothing behind the couch. As my eyes dart around, searching for any sign of where it might have gone, I see Aaron leaning over the back of the couch looking down at me.

"Whoa, you see a ghost in here?" He rubs his jaw, red and slightly swollen, and glances back over his shoulder. "This movie too much? I'll take it out of the rotation if you want."

Aaron's never put me down for my magic before, but the way he asked the question . . . He's definitely making fun of me.

I see his phone dangling in his hand, the screen still black, but a small green light on the top flashes to indicate a text.

He has every right to make fun of me. I don't even know why he bothers with me anymore.

I ruin everything.

As I stand, I take a long, deep breath.

"I think I need to go home," I say.

Aaron looks concerned—or feigns it, I can't tell—but nods. He brushes me off with a wave when I offer to get him some ice for his quickly swelling jaw.

"I got it," he assures me, but then he frowns. "Gemma, you've seemed kind of, uh, on edge lately. Do you think maybe you want to look into seeing one of those—"

"I'm fine," I interrupt, trying hard to focus on anything

but the flashing light on his phone. Someone is clearly waiting to hear from him. I'm just being a bother. Through a tightening throat, I repeat, "I'm fine."

"Geez, okay," he says, opening the door as I pull on my shoes. As I step out, he adds, "Let me know when you get home safe."

What, so you know I'm as far away as possible? The thought rises unbidden, and I'm still trying to shoo it away when the door closes behind me.

The rain batters the door to the apartment building as I step outside and into the night. I search the hazy trees for a sign of *the* shadow, but every shadow looks spooky tonight, and I wouldn't be able to pick out one following me if I tried.

So I don't. I slide onto my bike and pedal as fast as I can toward home, as if I could outride the curse chasing after me.

Another stray thought chases me too, as I blink rain and tears from my eyes.

If Aaron doesn't want me around anymore, why would he keep inviting me to movie night? To keep an eye on me? To watch the fallout?

To see what his curse has wrought?

Aaron's part of a whole non-magical family. But he knows plenty of other magical people, people that would—and have—cast spells for him if he asked. Would Aaron go that far, though, to get back at me for ruining a months-long relationship?

I think back to the blinking light on his phone, and my stomach drops once more.

I wouldn't blame him, I guess, if he did.

Eight

SATURDAY AFTERNOON

The table is set: three candles at each point of a triangle drawn in chalk with a new set of runes surrounding it, little piles of salt lining the whole setup like a pearl necklace.

"Okay?" I ask the empty room. Two floors up, I hear the closet doors rattling. "That was literally not a question for you!" I call up to them. The rattling continues. Fine, whatever.

I pull a scrap of paper covered in scribbles out of my pocket, take a deep breath, and start reading out loud. The spelled words slip over my tongue like cool water, and the candles flicker in response. I speak words of dispelling, words of freedom, words of moving on. I'd been working on this one before my suicide mission and wasn't happy enough with it to try it, but hey, since dying didn't work, can't hurt to give this a go now!

I reach the end of my scribbles and let out a slow, calm breath. The rattling upstairs has stopped for the moment. The candles flicker one more time, then go out all at once.

68

"Yeah?" I ask hopefully.

The shadow creature launches up through the table, imitating one of those kitschy Halloween jump scare machines, and I cover my face with my arms. The salt piles are flung into the air. I can taste it on my tongue as I breathe, feel it settling in my throat, drying me out from the inside.

I rush to the sink and turn on the water, cupping my hands and taking quick gulps to wash away the grittiness, then cough to get my lungs back in working order.

When the sodium-rich dust settles, I crumple my scrap paper into a ball and throw it into the sink. Muscle memory takes over long enough for me to reach toward the shelf above the breakfast nook before my brain catches up and I remember—

Empty. Everything is empty. The shelves where I used to keep my notebooks for writing spells and the little cup that held my favorite writing pen. The table that once housed a small collection of tarot decks stacked around the little circle of space I cleared out to try my hand at embroidery in a fit of inspiration brought on by Miss Tess and a spool of sparkling thread. The cabinet once stuffed with my favorite snacks. For a moment, it's jarring seeing all the space, all the air where things should be.

I did that. I put everything away, out of sight. Because the sight of anything, any bit of clutter, any unexpected shadow, scared the shit out of me.

There are things in my house, but I made it feel hollow.

It's the curse's fault. I jump at every shadow, hold my breath for something to fall off a shelf and shatter at my feet. The suspense kills me. So I tried to kill it first.

Now? Now it makes me feel . . . itchy. Like a sweater

that's too warm, made of wool that's barely rough enough to notice. It's just wrong.

I miss the comfort of clutter. Shelves stacked with books and cups full of pens and tables buried in craft supplies, unread mail, junk I never have the time to put away.

Had. Never *had* the time to put away. Until I absolutely had to.

The wind whistles through the trees outside, and I turn to look out the window in the front door.

It's there. The shadow. For a second, it's among the trees, then it's in the yard, then—

It's right outside the door.

It doesn't come any closer. But it doesn't have to. It's frozen the blood in my veins from there. I can almost feel how much it knows it. The taste of salt still coats my tongue.

Mission accomplished, I think. *Time for you to go home.*

But it doesn't. Because it's already home.

Nine

SUNDAY NIGHT

I'm outside again. It's dark. It's raining. The raindrops hit my bare arms in icy pinpricks, only a few degrees short of being stinging hale. I suppose I should enjoy the sensation while I can. There's no coming back from what I'm about to do.

This time, I lock the door. I don't know how long it will take anyone to find me, and I don't relish the idea of someone being able to get in and wreck my family's house before someone who cares discovers it's empty.

They're going to be enough of a wreck when they realize what I've done.

Or maybe they won't. Maybe this will be better for everyone.

I step onto the mushy ground, amazed that my feet don't sink straight into the earth, between the leaves and into the mud. It could just swallow me whole, and there I'd lay, buried under the same house that raised me, never to be raised again.

They could try, but the ghosts of necromancers are notoriously difficult to call back once they've passed through the Veil. Supposedly, we get too at home on the other side.

And me? Once I'm gone, I don't ever want to come back here.

Onward I go, my feet carrying me down the same path I've trod hundreds of times. I don't hum or tap on the instrument in my hand. The sound of the pelting rain is enough for me.

The human brain can keep going for a bit after every other organ has failed. Assuming it wasn't the thing that was hurt, the last spark of life in your body may well be your mind struggling to get everything back in order.

I'm going to cut that possibility off at the pass. I'm going out brain-first this time.

I hear the shadow skulking along in my wake as I trudge through the trees. Its footfalls squelch in the mud, and its appendages rustle the branches above, sending even more raindrops straight down upon me. When did it get so foggy? I can almost see my breath, and I can more than almost feel each damp lungful being pulled in and pushed out. I'm walking at a normal pace along relatively even ground, but suddenly, it feels like I'm running uphill.

I'm damp with rain and sweat by the time I reach my tree. My little arch, my imagined fairy doorway. My gaze catches again on the spot directly below the arch's zenith. How many times did I land there after jumping from the highest point, sure that it was some great feat of athleticism, leaving my own footprints in the dirt behind me like some kind of monster?

I glance around for my ever-present companion. It moves around the clearing, but I can't see it here. It hasn't left a single footprint in the muddy earth nor broken a single branch that I can home in on.

"Fucker," I mutter. Then, louder, "Coward. Only want to show yourself when I'm not looking for you? Come out, come out, wherever you are!"

I lift the gun with both hands. It's a handgun, nothing fancy—not that I know a lot about guns, but it was very cheap and upsettingly easy to get. I hold it out in front of me, one hand supporting the other, my finger resting on the trigger guard. If cop shows have taught me one thing, it's that you're not supposed to put your finger on the trigger until you're ready to shoot. And that this is how you hold a gun, arms outstretched and at face height. Taught me two things, then.

What they did not teach me was how to effectively provoke a curse creature. Despite my taunts, it does not appear. After a few minutes, when my hands start to shake and my vision blurs with the rain, I realize I can't even hear it moving around anymore.

It's gone quiet.

Is it waiting for something?

I drop my arms. The weight of the gun drags heavily, and it almost slips from my wet fingers.

Oh. It's waiting for me.

"Fine. Is this what you wanted?"

I lift the gun. Press the barrel to my temple. Bring my finger from the guard to the trigger.

"Tell whoever sent you that this is over. That they can leave me and my friends alone now. They got what they wanted. They win."

There's no response. Even the rain, which I can still feel

dropping onto my head and dripping down my back in tickling rivulets, seems to go silent.

I feel my finger tighten on the trigger, then, blessedly, nothing else.

I'M IN THE DARK AGAIN.

I don't open my eyes. I'm still half-awake, right? If I keep my eyes closed, I can keep dreaming, drift back to sleep, never wake up again . . .

But I am awake. Every second of awareness brings this fact more fully into focus. My heart beats, my lungs inflate, and if I'm noticing all these things, my brain is somehow still in one piece.

Or maybe this is my last gasp? Am I feeling myself go?

I lay there for what I'd guess is a few more minutes—time is fucky behind the Veil—before admitting defeat. My muscles, for all they ache, still respond when I tell them to sit me up. My lids still lift when I order my eyes open.

"God. Damn it."

The glowing eyes blink slowly from across the space. I couldn't say in any earthly terms how far away they are, but they are closer than they were before.

They stare at me, little spheres of static, raising the hairs on my arm and the back of my neck.

"What more could you possibly want from me? Aren't curses supposed to drive people to hurt themselves? Or is it not enough that I hurt the people around me too?"

Blink. Blink.

I groan. "Look, if you're holding my soul here to torture me, fine. I'm a medium, I go here sometimes. Just . . . leave my friends alone, okay? And my family? They're assholes, but we all are, right? It was me you wanted, so here I am." I raise both arms, then let them fall. When they hit what passes for "ground", they land with a mildly sticky *smack*.

Looking down at my lap, I add, "It's not as if I had anything left to do anyway. Everyone's pissed at me. All my projects have gone to shit. I can't find my fucking cards. My needles keep going missing, and I haven't written a functional spell in years. Really, I don't know why whoever sent you sent you to *me*. I was cursing myself way before you got here."

I look up.

The eyes are right in front of me. No tangible face holds them. No mouth for it to breathe through, but I feel the air move around me anyway, the cold exhale of something not alive, and more than that, *not right*. The eyes—they're glowing like miniature suns, and it hurts, ohfuckohmygod my head *hurts*—

PART TWO

Thoughts Still Clinging

Ten

MONDAY MORNING

I gasp, swinging both arms above me from my position flat on the moist earth.

Earth.

I'm on earth again.

No. Fuck no. No, no, *no*!

I slam my hands down on either side of me and kick both feet, splashing mud and leaves and sticks and rainwater onto my everything—all over my clothes, my face, into my open, screaming mouth. It slips, cold and bitter, over my tongue, and as I try to spit it out, the grit of dirt in my teeth makes me want to scream again.

I sit up, take a deep breath, then lean over and throw up as convulsions wrack my back, tensing every muscle at once. When I can finally breathe again, I have to sit for several minutes with my eyes closed, waiting for the nausea and dizziness to pass.

I look down at the mess, all but wishing to see something awful and magical having spilled out of me. I don't know what throwing up a curse looks like, but I'm hoping to find out.

Alas. What I find appears to have once been my dinner. Identifiable bits of carrot linger among the bile and—

A single spent bullet.

Nothing about this curse is normal. After a shower long enough to let the water run cold and a cup of tea to get the taste of regurgitated carrots out of my mouth, I think I know what's so wrong about it. As a necromancer, even a low-grade one, I've read plenty about curses since most *supposedly* stem from us. That's not really true, but the stigma does mean that most of the literature about curses is at least tangentially related to my field of magic. And there's one thing a lot of the most harmful curses have in common.

They're cast by non-magic folk.

One might think someone without magic trying to cast a powerful curse would result in nothing, but no, it's much more destructive than that. They don't even have to be trying for a curse to create one. Those born without magic can learn to wield bits of it for short periods of time with the right components. But if they do it wrong? Oh, someone's getting hurt.

Who's close to me but doesn't know how to use magic? Who's looked down on me for as long as I've had my magic? Who wouldn't want me dead but would want me miserable enough to drag my sorry carcass back, begging for relief and forgiveness?

The downside to giving your parents a key to your house

is that they can walk in whenever they want. The upside is that you can ask for the same courtesy.

It's 10 a.m. when I slam my parents' door open, startling them both out of their seats on the living room couch. My mom drops her book, and Dad nearly knocks his coffee mug off the side table.

"Gemma, honey, are you okay?" asks Mom, standing slowly, as if I'm a wild animal she doesn't want to send bolting. "We weren't expecting to see you until next—"

"What did you do?" I demand.

Dad stands up next, not nearly as carefully as Mom. "Gemma, what in the hell are you talking about?"

I stalk forward, my steps crashing into the floor, sending tremors up the walls. The family photos hung in the hallway shiver.

"I said: What. Did. You. Do."

They look at each other sidelong, and I know, I *know* they did this.

"Honey," Mom starts again, "what are you talking about?"

"Did you know that when a non-magic-user casts a spell, it can go wrong? Horrible, curse-levels of wrong?" They both stare at me blankly. The color in my dad's face rises with my every word. "Maybe you didn't realize before you cast something on me, but I'm telling you now: Whatever you did, you fucked it up. So, what was it? Were you trying to spell me a friend? Thought you'd try your hands at necromancy and got me stuck with a hanger-on? Or did you want to take my magic away entirely?"

Dad's cheeks puff out in indignation. "Who the hell do you think you are, barging into our house and making demands? You may be family, but I will not be spoken to like this in my own house."

I swear I only take one step, but suddenly, I'm in front of him with only inches between our flushed faces. He has the good grace—or the lack thereof—to look startled for a second before he regains his furious composure.

"I have been *cursed* by whatever you did for *months*. I am being followed, I am being harassed, I am being made to feel unsafe everywhere I go."

Mom reaches out as if to pat my shoulder, but at my flinch, she shrinks back. "Gemma . . ."

"I have tried counterspells. I have tried rearranging my life to make myself feel safe. I've stabbed myself in the heart and shot myself in the head, but whatever you've done has made it so that even the Veil doesn't want me!"

Out of the corner of my eye, I can see my mom's eyes glittering with tears, but my focus remains on my dad's face. It stays gruff for a moment, until the words sink in, until it occurs to him that I don't mean I've done all those things metaphorically.

I can practically hear the gears grinding in his mind, no doubt looking for a way to deflect, before he says, "Gemma, what on earth makes you think we'd want to cause you that kind of pain?"

The dodgeball hits me straight in the chest, and suddenly, all the anger I've held onto for years comes spewing out, tasting even worse than half-digested carrots on my tongue.

"You spoiled everything. You took the one thing I cared about, the one thing that made me *me*, and made it a fucking joke."

His eyes dart to my mom's, and she shakes her head. Of course they don't remember—nothing that's ever hurt me has ever really been that bad, or at least not bad or important enough to register in their minds. As if I'm making it all up. As if I'm just being dramatic.

Maybe I am. Maybe that's my right.

"Thanksgiving, 2013."

Dad's eyebrows scrunch, suggesting that he's thinking back, wondering what on earth could have happened on that night to make me this angry. More bile bubbles in my stomach. I hate that the moment that changed my life is probably nothing but another story he tells at work. A tale to laugh over after dinner.

The words burn up my throat. "The last year we hosted at the house. Gram was there, and Aunt Cara and too many little cousins for me to count. Everyone was finishing up dinner, and I guess you didn't have any more witty jokes to tell before people left, so you thought it would be fun to pull out one of my spell books."

This time, Mom does get a hand on my shoulder, but instinctively, my arm flies up to slap hers away. I turn to her, more and more angry that there are tears in my eyes when I say, "And you didn't stop him."

She shakes her head. Agreeing with my assessment? Implying she didn't know? Or that she couldn't have stopped him if she tried? It doesn't matter. What matters is that she didn't try. And . . .

I turn back to my dad, whose expression has finally gone from defensive to apologetic. The redness drains from his cheeks and rushes to his ears. He's not angry anymore, but he is embarrassed.

Good. Exactly like I was.

I take a stuttering breath into unstable lungs. "It's not that you read my spells out loud to everyone. I would have shared them if you'd asked; I was so proud of them. It's that you read them like they were a *joke.* Laughed and had everyone else laugh along as if none of my words, my work, mattered. And then you—" My throat constricts, and I have to swallow to get the last few words out. They come out as a question, like after all this time, I'm still asking, *Why?* "You looked at me like I was in on the gag? Like I'd also want to laugh at everything I'd ever created?"

His mouth opens and closes a few times, like he's chewing on possible words, until he finally settles on, "Honey, I'm so sorry."

"Yeah," I say, the burning in my chest going ice-cold. "Well, you fucking should be. Did you even notice when I stopped writing spells? That I never put pen to paper again while you and Mom lived in the house?"

I look between the two of them, and it's clear neither of them did.

The only thing I ever wanted to do with my life, the thing that made me happiest, my power to actually create something with my small amount of magic . . . and it had never even occurred to them that I'd stopped doing any of it while in their presence. I couldn't bear to because, what if they saw it? What if they shared it? What if it was all still a joke?

For years, even after they'd moved out, every time I looked at one of my beautiful notebooks, I got queasy. Every time I picked up a pen, even my very favorite pen with the perfect grip and the smoothest ink, my hands shook. All I could think about was how little it all meant. How even the best of what I did wasn't worth more than a laugh over dinner. *Have you heard Gemma's latest? Too funny!*

And now, with the curse, it's as if they never let it go.

Like they'd already tainted what I loved most and still felt the need to take the last scrap of it away.

The tears spill over and are dripping down my face. A part of me wants to run to my mom, hug my dad, let them make this all better. That's what parents are supposed to do, right?

Mom walks slowly to Dad's side and takes his hand. "Gemma," she says carefully, "I'm so sorry."

And they look it. Truly, they do. It doesn't even seem as though Dad's got a retort this time. No defense against his daughter who he hurt without a thought. Without really meaning to.

Without . . .

They didn't curse me. Either of them. The worst pain they ever caused me was inadvertent.

I swallow hard and wipe my face. "I'm sorry too," I say past a sob.

They look like they want to reach out and hug me, but I cannot possibly handle that right now, so I rush back to the door and close it on my way out. I throw myself onto my bike and launch myself forward, letting the incoming wind dry my damp cheeks.

It's not raining, but the clouds are rolling in.

We're in for a storm.

The most magical place in town is the Embroiderie, if only for the sheer volume of Crafting knickknacks crammed into the store. It stands to reason that the most magical place in town would also harbor one of the most magical people. Someone with enough power to cast a spell I couldn't sense until it was already haunting me, until it was too late to take it back.

The ache of exhaustion pulses in every one of my joints as I climb off my bike in front of the shop. The first drops of rain patter down as I lean my bike on the side of the building and push my way through the door.

The heater is on, buzzing away and blowing lukewarm air across my damp skin. I look past the myriad displays to my little corner, my hanging curtain. Something like safety shimmers behind it. Or at least, I think that's what it is until Miss Tess creeps out from the shadows, my tablecloth and incense burner in hand.

"Why?" I say. I mean it to come out more as a demand, but it's hardly a gasp when it clears my lungs.

Miss Tess always knows what's happening in her shop. Whether that's magic or just years' worth of intuition, I'm not sure. But she looks at me now, her mouth drawn into a guilty frown.

"Gemma, I'm—What are you doing here? You're not due in until tomorrow."

I huff. It's almost a relief. Of course *she* did this to me.

"You have to stop. Please. I need it to stop."

She adjusts the weight of the items in her hands, shifting from foot to foot and glancing around as if she's looking for somewhere to put my things. My curtain still hangs open, and I can see that my little round table has been pushed into the corner fully, chairs stacked neatly on top of it, as if it's closing time at a café.

Miss Tess finally gives up her search for clear space and sets the bundle in her hands onto the floor.

When she straightens, her frown has been replaced by a thin-lipped look of resolve.

"You know why," she says, gesturing to my curtain. "It's time for a change, Gemma. It's been time for a while now."

"A change?" I ask. "You fucking cursed me because, what, you got tired of not having more shelf space? Are the tarot displays more important than what I do here?"

Her face crumples, her brow furrowing and head tilting a bit. "Cursed? Honey, I told you I was going to have to move things around back here." She sighs. "You know I value what you do, but sometimes—"

"Take it back."

"What?" Her head tilts the other way, reminding me of a dog trying to hear better.

"Take it back," I say louder. "The curse. Turn it off,

dispel it, get it off me, and I'll do whatever you want." My breath catches on the last word.

At that, she straightens. "Curse? Like, for real? Oh, Gemma, I thought you were just playing it up for your ambiance. What's happened?" She steps forward, inexplicably smoothly for someone making their way through a labyrinth of yarn baskets and rock garden supplies. She's almost to me, her hands outstretched and aiming for my shoulders, before I finally move.

"Stay back!" I push over one of the tables in front of me, the one displaying packets of seeds ready for planting. Or, at least, that's what I meant to do. But instead, three tables go flying in three different directions. Seeds and scented markers and multi-colored spools of thread fly everywhere.

Miss Tess stops, her hands still held out but now flat, shielding herself.

"Gemma," she says, "tell me what's wrong."

"You know what's wrong!"

If it wasn't my parents who cursed me, it had to have been Miss Tess. She's got more than enough tools at her disposal, years of practice on both offensive and defensive spells, and—

Okay. I deserve to be cursed by her, the only person who I've ever permanently disfigured with my magic.

I remember sitting behind my curtain, having just watched a pair of displeased customers leave. Miss Tess stared back at me from the register. Somehow, she seemed both miles away and only inches from me.

I was sure she was going to fire me. One more failure to add to the list

I closed my eyes and held my breath and counted to ten, to twenty, to thirty-five—

Footsteps came toward me, then right next to me. "Gemma, we need to talk."

I panicked. I meant to stand and walk out before she could land the final blow. I did not mean to land a blow of my own. The moment I stood, all the air in the room rushed away from me. It blew my curtain out so far, the curtain rod strained. The tables on either side of my little booth toppled.

Miss Tess screamed.

When I opened my eyes, she lay on the floor in front of my table, glasses off, one hand pressed to her left ear. She was gasping for breath, shaking. When she lifted that hand, I saw blood. A second later, I saw the rounded top of her ear.

On the floor. Next to her bloody glasses.

"I'm sorry," I say on a staggered breath. "I know what I did to you was wrong. I know I'll never be able to really pay you back. But, Miss Tess . . . do you want me dead?"

Her hands drop to her sides, seemingly in defeat. "Gemma, hon . . . What happened was an accident. I don't want you dead for it, good lord."

"Then you just want me to suffer?"

"No, I don't want that either."

"Then take it back," I beg. I press my hands to my stomach and feel my lungs struggle to inflate. "Please, I can't keep doing this. I've tried to undo it myself, but I can't find the right spell and my pen is gone and dying hurts *so much*."

She doesn't say anything. Instead, she adjusts her glasses and calmly zig-zags her way past me, keeping several displays between us as she goes. I track her progress until she makes it to the front register and lays her palms flat on the counter. The Okay Conjunction waves in the draft from the heater.

"Gemma," she says finally, and my stomach churns waiting for the final condemnation. "I am willing to help you fix whatever has happened, but you need to explain it to me first."

"Don't lie to me." I mean to stomp angrily toward the counter but can only manage to wobble past tables and shelves. "Please, for fuck's sake, if you're mad at me, then be mad. Do it to my face, please, I am so tired . . ."

Her nails tap on the wooden countertop. "I'm not mad."

"Then get mad!" I shove a spinning rack of charms, which fall to the floor with a jarring chime like a dinner bell gone wrong. "I'm mad! You should be mad! Just get mad and get it over with!"

Her look of patience never wavers, but her nails click even faster the closer I get to the register. She says again, "I'm not mad. And I don't know what's happened to you, but if you want to sit down and tell me—"

"Don't. Lie. To. Me."

She steps back, pressing a hand to the bottom of The Okay Conjunction, and I can feel it go to work. A calming aura passes over me, and for a moment, every ache in my body begs me to sit down, to drop onto the carpet and stop moving for a bit.

Fuck no. I'm not about to be dissuaded by a tangle of thread uglier than the road to my house.

We're ending this here.

I raise both hands as if to bring them down on the counter where hers were, but instead, I bring the air in the room up with the motion. Flyers and postcards fly off the nearby counters and obscure my view of Miss Tess, the door, everything more than an arm's length away. I reach for her, meaning to take her by the shoulders and shake the truth out of her.

The impact running up my arms is less physical and more

magical, though. It's the same kind of pressure I feel when I'm pushing through the Veil to find a difficult soul, but more sudden and jarring than it's ever been. I pull back and press my hands under my arms to stop the jittery feeling of my bones shaking.

The air stops rushing, the papers fall to the floor, and the room goes silent.

When I can see again, I notice the Conjunction is gone. Only a few tattered threads still hang from the ceiling above the register. I don't see Miss Tess. Maybe she fell. Maybe she's right behind the counter, laying amongst the tattered wreck of her life's work.

Or maybe I just pushed her directly beyond the Veil, where no living soul is meant to be.

I deal with the dead as a rule. The impressions left behind when the body goes to rot. Oh god, is Miss Tess rotting right now?

I lean over the counter, arms wrapped tightly around myself. I'm afraid to touch anything. I'm afraid to even breathe.

The Tess-shaped lump on the other side of the counter isn't moving. I should get closer, make sure she's okay, but my vision goes blurry at the thought, and I panic. This time, I don't stay and help. This time, I run.

Twelve

My stomach heaving and head spinning, I stumble through the door and out into the rain.

Did I just kill someone?

Giant raindrops splatter against the pavement, battering my face. I can hardly see. But who needs vision? Vision is a crutch. Maybe it's better to not see at all.

I fall. My knees slam painfully on the sidewalk. I don't know how far I've come. It couldn't have been far, but I can't see. Everything's a haze of gray, and my stomach is still deciding whether or not to rebel and now my knees hurt and—

"Gemma?"

Aaron. I try to answer him, I really do, but it feels like I'm choking on my own tongue, so all that comes out is a wet cough as I try to clear my throat.

I feel him kneel down next to me, his warm hand gripping my sopping wet arm. "Gemma, are you okay?"

I don't know. I might have killed Miss Tess. Just thinking the words makes me dizzy again, and I press both hands to my face, covering my eyes and applying pressure. Stars burst in my vision.

"Okay," Aaron says, barely contained panic slipping through. "Okay. Let's . . . Okay."

He gently grabs my elbows and pulls me up. I follow his silent instruction and stand, eyes still covered. He leads me away, possibly from the scene of a crime, and I try to get the words out, to warn him that this might make him an accomplice. I don't know, the most experience I've ever had with the law is the true crime side of YouTube. But he keeps leading and I keep letting myself follow, and it all seems so useless now.

We're several turns down the road before I finally take my hands away from my face enough to see where we're headed. The library. Of course. What kind of murderer would hide out in a library? The perfect hiding place until I can get my bearings. Or until Aaron can call the police, which would be more than fair.

He ushers me inside and directs me into one of the chairs in the newly renovated and weirdly symmetrically-organized meeting room. Four circular tables sit in the center, each surrounded by exactly four chairs set at equal intervals. The tables are empty and freshly cleaned, the faux-wood shining in the light of the fluorescent bulbs above, and the chairs are the awful plastic kind that pinch if grabbed the wrong way. If I focus on the bumpy plastic texture of the one I'm sitting in I won't have to think about The Embroiderie and Miss Tess and—

"I think I'm gonna throw up."

Aaron disappears from my line of sight only to reappear a

second later with a small trash can, which he sets in front of me. I lean over it as my stomach churns, waiting.

Another set of footsteps pad across the rough carpet behind me. They don't speak, but from my prone position, I can see Aaron's feet shift as he acknowledges the person, maybe trying to get them to leave.

They don't leave, though, instead stepping farther into the room. My nauseated stomach nearly drops out entirely when I recognize the sneakers that come into view.

"Gem?" Callie asks softly. "Are you okay?"

I shake my head, less to indicate a "no" and more in an attempt to shoo her away. I don't want either of my best friends being counted as accomplices to whatever I've just done.

"Miss Tess looked a little banged up," Aaron says. "But Gemma seems really shaken. I can't tell if she's hurt or . . ."

"Miss Tess," I say. "Is she . . . ?"

"Here?" Aaron finishes. "No, she stayed back at the shop. A lot of stuff was all akimbo in there. What happened?"

I look up so quickly, I have to blink away a bout of dizziness. Aaron and Callie both lean on the table in front of me with matching looks of confused concern furrowing their brows and pulling frowns across their cheeks.

"She's . . . She's not dead?"

At that, Aaron raises an eyebrow. "No, she's not dead! God, Gemma, did someone break in? Some*thing*? What did you think killed her?"

I gulp the feeling of bile back down my throat. "Me. I thought I killed her."

Aaron still looks confused, but Callie starts wringing her hands together nervously. She knows about the first incident with Miss Tess. She knows why I'd be worried about having hurt her even worse this time.

"Let me get you some water, okay?" she says, then pushes off the table.

Aaron crosses his arms and sighs. Then his phone goes off, and he pulls it from his pocket immediately, turning away from me as he answers it. "Hey. No, it didn't work the way you said. Look, I have to go. I'll be home later. I'll call you when I'm on the way. Okay, I—you too."

He swipes to end the call and slips the phone back into his pocket so quickly, I wouldn't have seen it happen at all if I hadn't been staring at him in icy horror.

Who was he talking to? What didn't work the way they said it would?

"Hey."

I nearly jump out of my skin when Callie sets a hand on my shoulder. She holds a small plastic cup of water in front of me, and I take it in my shaky hands. Then she returns to her post at the table next to Aaron, watching me closely. "Okay. So. What happened?"

Where would I even begin to explain? Miss Tess? My parents? The curse?

The curse. I should start with the curse.

So I do.

I explain the last six months, starting with the sleepless nights, the growing paranoia, and eventually the actual, visible shadow-being that's been following me around. I remind them of a few times I've reacted to it in their presence —apologizing again to Aaron for the bruise on his chin, which he waves away—and by the time I reach the part about Miss Tess, I've caught the two of them exchanging glances more than once. Too many times for my own comfort.

"What?" I demand when I catch them doing it again at the mention of The Okay Conjunction unraveling.

Callie winces, then asks, "Why didn't you tell anyone?"

"That I was being followed by a shadow thing no one else can see? That I'm pretty sure I'm cursed even though I can't prove it? I don't know, how well do you think that would have gone over?"

"Just fine," Aaron chimes in, "if you'd have said something before you went completely off the handle about it."

It's my turn to cross my arms. "I'm on the handle. I've never been more securely on the handle. But the handling has to be done by me and the person who cursed me, because no one else can even see what's happening and—and no one else should have to get hurt."

Callie squats in front of me, her left knee crunching loudly as she goes, though she doesn't show an ounce of discomfort. She reaches forward and sets her hands on my knees, as much to steady herself as to reassure me. She squeezes lightly.

"Gemma, you shouldn't have to face this alone. You can't keep *actually* hurting yourself just so someone else *maybe* doesn't get hurt."

"There's no maybe about it, though," I say, setting my cold hands on top of her warm ones. Gods, how does she do that? "Miss Tess is hurt right this second, and this isn't the first time. Plus, I nearly hurt you and I *did* hurt Aaron and—"

It happens in a second, all at once, as if it's been waiting for a quiet moment to strike. Aaron pulls his phone out and types quickly; Callie's phone vibrates in her pocket. She glances at it, then back up at Aaron; and as their eyes meet, the shadow rises from behind one of the tables. It reaches its dark, smoky, burning arms across the space toward the three of us.

I jump to my feet, pulling Callie's hands, and she falls forward, her head slamming into my knees. I back up and away from the shadow, dragging Callie along the carpet.

"Ow, Gem, stop!" she says, yanking her hands free.

She drops like an angry sack of potatoes. She rolls to the side—away from me, the threat, I realize—and comes up on her knees, her hands held in front of her defensively. Or placatingly? She's scared of me in either case, and I wouldn't blame her, except—

"Aaron!" I lunge back, grabbing the chair I'd been sitting in and swinging it over my head as the shadow rises over the tables and looms above my best friend.

He flinches, hands raising as if to catch the chair, and I manage to swing it around so it flies over his head and into the shadow. Into and through, slamming into the shelves along the back wall and scattering books across the floor. The shadow stops reaching for Aaron, but it's clearly not hurt.

"Move!" I scream, shoving Aaron. He yells something that I don't hear as I clamber onto the table next to the shadow. If it were a ghost, I'd try to force it back through the Veil with a spell I've used once or twice on particularly stubborn spirits who found their loved ones once again and refused to let go.

This is different, though. Instead of the chilly fog of a spirit, touching the shadow feels like plunging my hands into lukewarm bath water. If not for the dark whisps coming off it with my every swipe and the ache in my arms as I swing, I'd think the thing wasn't even really here at all.

The shadow vanishes. I turn on my heel, checking every corner of the room frantically in case it's just hiding, but no, it really seems to be gone. On my last turn around the room, one foot catches on the other, and I fall to my knees on the hard plastic of the table. I hear the metal of one of the legs snap, and the table tilts, sending me sprawling onto the floor.

I go limp and let it happen. The room is silent except for the sounds of three people breathing heavily.

When I confirm my heart isn't about to beat directly through my ribcage and onto the carpet, I sit up and look for Aaron and Callie.

They're on the other side of the room, next to the door, as if they were about to bolt. They should have. Had they even seen that thing? It could have taken us all out!

Wait. *Had* they seen that thing?

I meet Aaron's gaze and ask, "Hey, are you guys okay?"

Immediately, Aaron's expression goes dark. He stomps toward me, face going a deeper shade of red with every step. "Are we *okay*? Gemma, what in the actual fuck was that about?"

Well, there's my answer. "The shadow thing," I answer. "It was right behind you, and—"

"Dammit, Gemma, what is *wrong* with you?"

I close my mouth so fast, I feel my teeth clamp together.

But he's clearly not done. "There was no fucking shadow monster. You are losing your damned mind and you won't even admit it! We have been trying to be nice about it, but for fuck's sake, you're hurting us!"

I open my mouth to defend myself, to say it was only to protect them, but Aaron has started pacing, and I now see that he's holding his shoulder—the one I threw the chair over. It must have hit him. I must not have thrown it high enough. My tongue stumbles over an apology.

Callie inches forward, though she seems reluctant to

approach. "Hey," she says quietly, "don't worry about me, it's a little rug burn, I'll—"

"No!" Aaron interrupts, stopping and turning to her. "No, don't do that. It wasn't a little anything. She freaked out. She could have hurt both of us. She could have . . ."

He gulps like he's trying to physically swallow the words back down, but I hear them anyway.

Killed them. I could have killed them.

A deep hollowness settles into my chest. This was the exact thing I wanted to protect them from, and I could have done it anyway. Without a thought. Three people I could have killed tonight.

And none of them deserve it.

I climb to my feet, keeping my hands at my sides, as non-threatening as possible. "I'm sorry. I should go."

"Go where?" Aaron demands. "Christ, Gemma, why are you always doing this? Why can't you sit down for five minutes and figure something out without making it a whole scene?"

I knew it. I knew he hated me. How long has he felt this way? How much of this has he been holding back, waiting to throw it all at me while I'm at my lowest?

Suddenly, the hollowness is replaced with the same fury I'd thrown at my parents and then at Miss Tess. Some part of me knows Aaron doesn't deserve it, but a larger part of me screams that I don't either.

"*I* need to figure something out? You wouldn't have gotten any of your own shit figured out without me!"

Aaron laughs, and I feel the knife in my chest all over again. "Seriously? Gemma, you're a great friend, but don't go pretending I owe my whole life to you. You need way more help than I ever have."

"Which is why you needed me to tell you March was a dick, huh?"

"Whoa, whoa, whoa, let's back up here, folks," Callie says, placing herself between us. She's limping hard. The side of her leg is scraped, a spot on her knee rubbed pink, nearly bleeding and beginning to swell. "We do not need to be bringing old wounds into this."

"I knew it," Aaron spits, ignoring Callie. "You said something to him, didn't you?"

I shake my head. "I didn't say shit. You ruined that all by yourself."

"Guys."

Aaron points an accusing finger at me. "You never liked him, and you didn't even know him! You were just jealous I was spending more time with him than with you!"

I curl my hands into fists.

"Guys!"

"You couldn't stand that I got to be happy with anyone else. It's you or no one, right?"

"Shut the fuck up," I hiss.

"You rely so much on other people, and you're still somehow so fucking lonely. How does that even work, Gemma? Can't rely on us, can't rely on yourself. What are you even doing?"

"*Guys!*"

"I don't know!"

I fling my arms out, meaning to gesture helplessly at the nothing that he's called me out for being. But instead of nothing, everything releases, every pent-up worry I've ever had about our friendship, my own life, myself—it all whooshes outward in a wave. Both Aaron and Callie are flung backward. Aaron trips over one of the tables, sliding all the way across and to the other side and hitting the floor with a *thump*. Callie is thrust to the side, onto her injured knee, and tries to catch herself on one of the chairs, but her hands slip, and she goes down too.

I'm breathing deep. My blood is pumping loudly in my ears. I hear a high-pitched whine, some kind of alarm. No, it's my own ears ringing.

I take a step toward them. I want to make sure that I didn't actually kill anyone this time.

Callie flinches away from me. Aaron groans from the other side of the table.

That's all I need, I guess.

I storm outside, into a storm. It's raining more than ever, dark and heavy, every inch of space between the raindrops wavering like my shadow creature.

Thirteen

I couldn't watch where I'm going if I wanted to, the rain is so thick. I'm practically swimming, but at least I know my way home through the muck.

Distantly, I wonder why there's no lightning, no thunder. There ought to be for a storm like this. But it's just rain and wind. Just the gush of buckets of water pouring onto the streets, battering the storefront windows, running in rivers down the gravel path, soaking every chilled inch of me and making the dark forest even darker. Darker than I think I've ever seen it.

When I was little, I used to stare out the window at the trees and imagine little creatures jumping and flying between them. Occasionally I'd catch something real—a squirrel, an owl, a bat—and almost convince myself I'd summoned it there by waiting.

That was before I'd known I was able to call on ghosts. At the time, being able to call bats would have excited me more.

But on the darkest nights, when the moon was nearly

new and I could only barely see the trees farthest from my window, I'd imagine something else. Not something jumping from tree to tree but something *becoming* the trees. A forested monster, making the silhouettes wave slowly against the night sky. Waving at me, maybe.

This cursed shadow? It's nothing like that.

It's anything but friendly and waving.

I finally arrive at the house, my house, where I grew up and hated everything I couldn't control until I could control it, and then I began to hate it in a whole new way.

Why didn't that fix everything? I thought independence was all I'd ever wanted, and it was for a while, but . . .

Why is it so lonely out here?

My eyes trail over the vines crawling up the side of the house, around the windows, all the way to the roof, scanning the dark twists and leafy turns as if there's a message to be found, the answer to my question written in the overgrown garden of my childhood home.

The rain hisses against the leaves of the trees behind me, sounding almost like footsteps, and I turn away from the house, eyes wide, watching for unnatural movement.

I see it.

Staring at me with its starry eyes. My shadow is waiting.

It can do whatever it wants. I'm done fighting.

The sounds of footsteps do not let up as I walk. They're asynchronous with my own and practically blend in with the patter of rain, but not quite. Not all the way. I step into the forest for the final time (for real, this time) and don't look back.

The arch waits for me like a parent with their arms crossed, looming and disappointed. And there's something at its feet—at its roots—a mound of mud, a little grave waiting just for me.

Is it mocking me? I feel like it's fucking mocking me.

I stomp toward it, mud splashing everywhere, ready to plunge my hands into the muck and pull up whatever is buried there, whatever it is I put here to forget. Could it be the counter to the curse that I've been looking for? Why would I make myself forget that, though? Why—

"Gemma!" someone calls before I can drop to my knees and start muck-diving.

I turn back to see three figures, two stumbling toward me through the rain, the last gliding casually. Aaron and Callie. And my shadow.

I'm not afraid for them anymore. Not because I'm mad —though I am, in a deep way I can't seem to shake—but I'm pretty sure it's not going to hurt them. I thought about it a bit on the way here, insomuch as I was able to think at all. The shadow hasn't actually hurt anyone I'm around.

It's always been me.

If it's a curse, this whole time, it's been a curse meant to trip me up, make me hurt the people I love most.

I look at Aaron and Callie and, god, I do love them.

This time, I'm glad they're here to see me go. Maybe that's been the missing ingredient all along. I can't continue to run away from my problems in secret. If life's going to let me go, there's got to be someone living to see it happen, a witness to my demise. I'm a bridge between the dead and the living, so they must be a bridge for me.

I'll cross them one last time, and then I'll go for good.

They get within arm's reach of me before I lift my hands

to bring them to a halt. I'm prepared to use magic, but they stop all on their own.

"Don't hurt yourself," Callie gasps. "Please don't. We can help—or get you help, or—something!"

My shadow is yards behind them, looming. And then it's closer, only a few feet away, then inches, and then—then it's everywhere. Every flash of light, every breeze through the branches, every raindrop flipping a leaf from side to side, it's there.

I try my best to keep my cool. It's trying to provoke me into hurting my friends one more time. I take slow breaths, but the panic has settled into my bones and it's spreading. My hands begin to shake.

Then, as quickly as it started, the shaking stops. Callie has her hands around my wrists, holding them still. She's so warm.

And I'm so cold. I'm battered and bruised and I can still feel the phantom ache of the knife in my chest, the hole in my head, scars I can't soothe, like everything else around me.

Wait.

I brought myself back from those things. From the dead. That's a level of necromancy I've never been able to achieve, shouldn't even be *able* to achieve based on my skillset.

I'm magical. I'm powerful.

If I can't break this curse, I'll tear it out of myself like a bullet, like a sharp knife.

I pull my wrists free of Callie's grasp and wrap my arms around myself, one across my chest to my shoulder and one around my stomach to my hip, and breathe deep.

"Gemma, what are you doing?" demands Aaron, and it takes everything in me to block him out. I'm doing this for him as much as I am for me. So he's safe. So we're all safe.

Aaron steps up beside Callie and mutters in her ear, saying she's got magic, she'd understand better, that she has to do something to snap me out of it.

But neither of them understand. Not the pain I'm going through, not the curse I'm suffering from, and not my magic. Not any of it.

I close my eyes and gather folds of the Veil around me as if they're my little curtain at the Embroiderie, shrouding me, coating me in deathly magics. I probe the way I would for a spirit on the other side. Only this time, I'm not probing outward; I'm probing inward, inside myself.

I search for the thing that's wrong, the thing that doesn't fit. The spit of magic that's been haunting me for too damn long. The thing that needs to get *out.*

And I find it. Like a clear marble in water, the last boba in a cup of tea, a little sphere of burning magic that radiates from my chest, right where my breathing has been stifled and my heart skips a beat every time I see that fucking shadow.

Callie's voice breaks through my concentration as she shouts, "Don't!"

"I have to," I gasp.

My eyes shoot open as her hand lands on mine, the one gripping my hip for dear life. Aaron steps forward and covers my other hand, his warmth seeping into the soaked shoulder of my shirt.

"Okay," says Callie, nodding. "You have to do this? Fine."

"But not alone," Aaron adds. "You're gonna let us help."

The shadows press in on us from all angles, a dark, writhing cage, but all I can feel are Callie's fingers slipping between mine and Aaron's thumb pressing my knuckles. I should be afraid of hurting them, but I'm not. As long as they're here, holding on to me, supporting me, I'm not afraid of anything at all.

I bite my lip and close my eyes again. With every stitch of magic I have in me, I grab that little pearl of wrongness and I *pull*.

Instead of coming loose as I expect it to, it bursts. Blinding light emanates from the space between us, visible even though my eyes are still closed. Aaron shouts and turns his head away even as he shifts closer to me. Callie buries her face in my neck with a surprised hiss. I scream, not in fear but in relief as the pressure in my chest releases.

The light fades all at once. Spots dance behind my eyelids. I breathe easier than I have in months, or maybe longer, and then I collapse for the third and final time in front of the arch in the woods outside my home.

Fourteen

TUESDAY AFTERNOON

This time, there's no darkness. No starry eyes giving me the third-degree. I'm not cold. I'm not wet. And I'm not dead.

But I am confused.

I sit up and regret it instantly as my vision spins. But I still *have* vision, so that's a plus.

When I can see straight again, I recognize my room: my rumpled bed, my messy dresser, and my exhausted looking best friend sitting in my childhood rocking chair on the other side of the room. He meets my eyes, his face expressionless, and my vision goes blurry again as my own face crumples and tears flow down my cheeks.

"I'm so—"

"If you apologize," he interrupts, standing and coming to sit next to me on the bed, "I will leave."

I sputter for a moment, unsure what else to say if I'm not allowed to beg for forgiveness. Finally, I come up with a tentative, "Thanks for bringing me home?"

Aaron sighs, and I'm worried that's not what he

wanted either. But before I can think of something else, he pulls out his phone and shows me the screen. It's displaying a picture of Aaron and another guy I've never seen before, with dark hair, dark eyes, and almost blindingly white teeth, sitting next to each other in Aaron's car. I can see a bar in the background through the car window, one in the city we've been to a few times before, though not recently.

"His name is Taylor. We've been dating for three months, and I'm sorry I didn't tell you."

My brain seems to have short-circuited. If I was struggling for something to say before, I'm drawing a complete blank now.

Aaron's running his free hand through his hair, then he pulls his phone back and looks at the image on the screen, and his expression softens. He pockets the phone and looks back at me.

"I'm sorry I didn't tell you. I was just—I didn't want— Oh, man." He rubs his face with both hands, then mumbles through his fingers, "I was hoping Callie would be back by now . . ."

I sniff, the tears having mostly but not entirely abated. "If you don't want to talk to me, I understand. You don't have to."

"No!" he insists. "I do! Want to, I mean. I'm . . . Ugh." He drops his hands and meets my gaze again. "I knew March was a dick. And I was so pissed. Pissed that *you* knew he was a dick and pissed that you knew it first. Like I was some dumbass kid with a crush too oblivious to figure it out for myself. So when I met Taylor, I was worried that . . . that you'd see something I didn't again, and I'd be the dumbass *again*, and that would suck because I *really* want you guys to get along. He's really nice, and he likes some of my favorite movies, and he's actually into tarot and—"

"Wait, wait, wait," I say, rubbing at my puffy eyes. "You have a new boyfriend. And you didn't want to tell me about him. Because you thought I'd think he was a dick?"

Aaron nods slowly, reluctantly. "It sounds dickish when you say it that way, but yeah."

I knew it, I *knew* he was hiding something! Some*one*, even! And he figured I'd ruin his relationship again, so of course he'd rather have a whole other second life instead of just telling me—

Wait, no. He said I was right about March. So he wasn't worried I'd ruin anything. He was worried this new guy would.

"Hey," I say, "that's not fair. To me or him."

"Yeah, I know."

I sniff again, breathing easier by the minute. "Then . . . can we have him over for movie night?" Aaron looks nervous about that. Movie night has been our thing for ages—not even Callie's been invited to join. But I don't budge, crossing my arms and nodding until he nods too. "I want to meet him. And I promise I'll warn you before I accuse him of being a dick. This time."

That earns a brief, bitter chuckle. "Yeah, okay."

We're quiet for a few minutes, and I drop my arms to fidget with my blanket.

Callie, bless her, joins us before I can make things weird again. When she comes in, her gaze travels from the rocking chair she clearly expected Aaron to still be in to the two of us on my bed. When she sees I've woken up and sat up, she rushes over and wraps both arms around me, nearly smothering me with her chest.

"You!" she says, pulling back suddenly, her hands still resting on my shoulders as if to hold me in place. "Don't you dare do anything like that to me ever again! Got it? The nerve!"

"Sorry."

"I'm not even upset about the library, but you bet your ass Nancy is, so you're coming in with me in a few days to help clean up. We will be on time—no, early! Got it?"

"Got it."

"And another thing!" She lets go of my shoulders and steps backward a few paces so she can lean on my dresser, her hands now on her hips. "I've made you an appointment with my mom's friend, Dr. Hawthorne, in the city. Two weeks from now. You're gonna go talk to her. Non-negotiable."

"Sounds like a date."

I'm doing my level best not to cry again. The fact that either of them are still talking to me, let alone trying to help me, is astounding. And Callie is quickly running out of hard-ass energy, as her hands fall to her sides and she bites her lip nervously.

"Also," she adds, looking away from me toward my window. "I called your parents."

My stomach sinks into the mattress. "Oh god, they're not coming here, are they?" I don't think I can handle that right now. Or maybe ever.

Thankfully, Callie shakes her head. "No, they're not coming here, and they don't expect you there for a while. They wanted me to tell you they said sorry and that they hope you'll come by when you can, at least to see Brett."

Oh. How . . . nice. This doesn't feel like a ping or dodge. For once, it feels kind of like an actual invitation, with a few less strings than usual attached. I feel about 20% less sick at the prospect of seeing them again, though if they're not going to slap a deadline on me, I don't think I'll be rushing back.

"Oh, and Miss Tess wants to talk to you," Aaron adds.

Callie shoots him a look, as if he wasn't supposed to say that, but I knew I would have to talk to her soon too. Sooner than my parents probably.

After all, I need to find out if I still have a job.

Fifteen

THURSDAY MORNING

There's no way I still have a job.

The shop is still a mess when I arrive two days later, having slept a lot more and woken to discover something—or rather, the lack of something.

My magic is gone.

Well, dormant. I've read about that happening to some magic-users right after they've cast something big. I can still feel my magic, right where it always is, but it's too depleted to actually make use of for a while. How long "a while" will be is the question.

Seems like my last stunt knocked out more than just the curse. I should be more upset, having lost something I thought was so vital to my very being, even temporarily. But I still feel like me without it. It's weird to think about, so I've been trying not to. The plus side is that I haven't seen any stalker shadows since, though I still jump like a spooked horse if I catch anything shady moving out of the corner of my eye.

Not trusting me to bike back into town yet, Aaron

brought me to the shop today in his car, a beat-up blue slug-bug, before heading to work himself. He even offered to go in with me, but really, I need to do this part on my own.

The bell over the door rings, and my feet land not on carpet but on paper. The pamphlets and postcards still litter the floor from my outburst. The tables I knocked over are still askew, their displays scattered and mixed amongst each other, so the whole scene resembles an *I Spy* book even more than usual.

Miss Tess pops up from behind the counter, her customer service smile slipping into something much more natural once she sees me. I expected her to be furious, to demand I take my things and go, but she doesn't look angry, just disappointed. And that hurts in a whole different way.

She takes a deep breath, then lets it out slowly. "Gemma. Thank you for coming by."

Oh lord. So formal. I am so fired.

Which is more than fair. I glance behind her to see that the shredded Okay Conjunction has been taken down from the wall. That's probably why she hasn't cleaned up the rest of the shop. A mess of shredded thread is no laughing matter. But it is, I'm sure, the last straw.

She's gearing up for some speech, and I let the words wash over me. She can't just fire me, she's gotta make a thing of it. That's fine. It gives me a few minutes to mentally say goodbye to this place. My eyes wander across the toppled tables, past the chaotic displays, over to my corner with my starry little curtain in my tiny little corner.

I'm going to miss that corner.

I was always anxious that my next fuck-up here would be my last, but I'm always anxious about everything. And who isn't worried about making a mistake at work? At least I knew Miss Tess would never dock my pay or cut my hours, even after . . . well.

She kept me on after that. Not as penance, I realize, not to keep reminding me what I did, but . . .

Without this job, I'd have been lost. What else do I even know how to do other than my middling medium tricks? Wash dishes? Make popcorn? I guess while my magic is out of commission, I'll need to do something like that. I need money if I'm going to keep the house—and keep myself fed. I wonder if the theater a few towns over his hiring?

"Gemma?"

I zone back in to Miss Tess. My ears are ringing a little when I ask, "Sorry, what did you say?"

"You're fired."

"Oh."

Yeah. That's about what I expected.

"Yep. Can't have a medium without magic. I mean, I could, but the customers are getting savvy these days with all these internet shows making shit look too easy. I don't think either of us want to put up with that."

I shake my head. The ringing is getting louder, so I clear my throat to try to drown it out. "Well, I guess then I'll . . ."

Her expression brightens suddenly, eyes going wide and smile crossing her cheeks like a crack in ice. "Hey, Gemma!" she says cheerfully as if this is the first time she's seeing me today. "I heard you're looking for a job!"

I squint at her incredulously. "Are you really making fun of me right now? That's kinda low."

The smile doesn't falter as she continues. "You know, it's been a while since we've had any new spells to cast on this place. Think you'd want to try your hand? I'd compensate you for your time, of course."

"I'm . . . What?"

Miss Tess looks sadly at the empty space where her tapestry once hung. The Okay Conjunction lies in tatters on the floor behind the till, the magic all bled out the moment the threads were cut.

"We are significantly less protected here now, and it's going to take me *ages* to rebuild the Conjunction. I'm gonna need some support in the meantime." She looks back to me without a scrap of bitterness, even though I'm the reason her magnum opus is frogged on the floor. If I didn't know any better, I'd say she even looks . . . excited? "Think you're up to the challenge of keeping this place intact?"

My hands disappear into the cuffs of my jacket as I try to hide the nervous fidgeting. How can she offer this after I just ruined everything?

"I don't know," I say weakly. "I'm not . . . I haven't written a working spell in years."

Miss Tess claps her hands together and nods. "How about I give you the basics of the spells I used, and you can build out from there? Use any components from the shop you need until your own power's up and running again."

"But . . . But this is all my fau—"

"Honey." Her hands fly apart and land solidly on my shoulders, and her eyes pin me in place. Even my fidgeting fingers still. "I can't say you don't hold any blame for the current state of things. But you also don't get to shoulder all of it. There's plenty I could have handled better too. But I'm betting nothing here is broken that can't be fixed. Or"—she shoots a glance at the pile of aida and embroidery thread behind the counter, her eyes aglitter at the challenge ahead—"remade."

I don't mean to. But I can't help it. One second, I'm

standing straight up, shocked and sad—and the next, I'm halfway to the floor, eyes drooping and breath hitching with exhaustion and something else.

I guess it's relief. Or maybe gratitude. Everything I wish I'd been aware enough to feel before now. Was it my magic blocking all of this?

No, not my magic. Me. I wasn't letting myself feel these things. Because I didn't deserve them.

I didn't *think* I deserved them.

Maybe I was wrong.

"Yeah, okay, let it all out," Miss Tess says quietly, patting me on the back as I hunch over, hands on my knees, trying to dispel the lump in my throat. "If it helps, I won't even make you sew the spells on. You won't have to touch a needle. In fact, I'd prefer it if you didn't."

Finally, a laugh escapes from between the sobs, and I can breathe again.

Sixteen

FRIDAY MORNING

The next morning, Callie is back bright and early to accompany me to the library. We're on cleaning duty for the next several days, which I apologize for until Callie says she'll be supervising and I'll be doing all the actual work. Which, yeah, fair.

"Oh, am I on suicide watch now?" I ask with a chuckle as she leans in my bedroom doorway, eyeing the clock on my wall.

She does not laugh back. She instead raises an eyebrow at me and states in no uncertain terms, "Yes."

I can't wipe the smile off my face, but I can acquiesce with a nod. That's also fair, I guess.

As we approach the front door, she scoops up my umbrella and holds it out to me. I take a look out the window: bright and sunny, only clouds of the cute and fluffy kind in the sky.

"Uh, thanks, but it's not raining?" I say.

Her face scrunches up, and she looks at the umbrella as if

she's seeing it for the first time. "Yeah, but I thought . . . Gem, you've been carrying this thing around for weeks."

"Yeah, because it's been *raining* for weeks."

"No, it hasn't."

It's my turn to look at her like she's crazy. "Yes, it has. Right up until the other night." I slip past her and point through the small panes in the front door. "Look at the garden, it's still a fucking mess, and the plants have all gone—"

I was going to say "bananas," but the word gets stuck in my throat as I look outside.

The plants are fine. Normal. A few of them even look a little dry, like they need some attention from the hose. I open the door and step outside, off the front step and onto—solid ground, flat ground, ground that hasn't been trampled by muddy boots at all lately. Turning back toward the house, I shield my eyes from the sun as I look up. The vines are whole, healthy, brown but not drooping as they would have been after weeks of heavy rain.

Was it like this yesterday? I don't even remember; I was so focused on my talk with Miss Tess . . . Everything could have settled overnight maybe. But having lived in this house all my life, I know the yard better than that.

I finally look back down, letting my eyes drift to Callie's. She's still standing in the doorway, umbrella in hand, looking at me like she's worried I'll bolt.

I don't. Instead, I laugh.

I laugh until my face is flushed and my sides hurt. It's a good ache, though, nothing phantom about it. Just plain old painful joy.

When I can breathe again, I look up to find that Callie

has finally come outside and shut the door behind her, but she still looks worried. I walk back to her and take one of her hands in mine.

"I'm fine. For real, this time," I say, giving her hand a squeeze.

I don't think she believes me, not entirely, but she squeezes back and gives me a small smile. "Let's get going. Nancy is going to flip if we're not there with brooms in hand by nine."

"Yeah, and it really takes a lot to get her riled up," I say sarcastically. Out of the corner of my eye, I see something shift in the trees, and I pause. It wasn't anything dark this time; instead, it was a flash of light, the sun peeking through the trees. "Hey. Will you come with me for a sec?"

She's already reaching for her bike, poised to hop on and pedal away. "Whyyy?" she asks, dragging the word out suspiciously.

"I think . . . I think I forgot something in there," I say, gesturing into the forest.

"No," she says immediately. "Nuh-uh, we are not going back in there for another crazy—"

"Nothing crazy," I say quickly, holding my hands up and meeting her gaze steadily, willing her to believe me. "I promise. It's . . . I just need a minute. And I'd really appreciate if you came with me. Please?"

The last word rushes out in a desperate sigh. I'm still practicing asking for support, and she's already doing so much, helping me heal and put everything I broke back together. But I need this. More than I need Nancy not to yell at me for tardiness.

More than maybe anything else I could possibly need in this moment.

I hold out my hand. She takes a deep breath, then sets her bike back against the house and drops her hand into mine.

"Five minutes," she says.

I nod. "Five minutes."

I lead her through the trees, along the path I've walked a thousand times, wearing my own trail into the low grasses. The ground here is solid too; not a bit of mud to be found under the layer of crunchy leaves. I make a mental note to bring that up later with someone who's got the right letters after their name to address it.

But for now, the late-fall breeze runs warmly through my hair, the sunlight shines warmly on my face, and Callie's hand sits warmly in mine. The cold in my bones has vacated to make room for something else.

We come to the arch in no time.

Like the other night, I look below it and see the corner of something sticking out of the ground, small enough that it might have been there all the time without me really seeing it. The closer I get to it, the more sure I am that that's exactly the case.

The dirt around the spot is smooth, meaning there has been at least *one* day of real rain since whatever it is was buried here. But even dry, it's easy to dig through with my hands.

Callie stands off to the side, looking more and more wary with each passing moment, until I finally unearth the treasure, and she gasps.

"I know that box!" she says with a smile. "Your junk drawer!"

I pout at her. "It's not a junk drawer! It's my memory box!"

She shrugs. "Same thing. Why'd you bury it out here? That's gotta be bad for the lace."

She's right. I turn the little wooden box over in my hands, examining the slightly rusty hinges on the back, the poorly painted flowers on the sides, and the formerly white lace hot-glued to the top. To be fair, it probably reached "formerly white" status a few years ago, but the dirt definitely did not help.

"Nothing I can't fix up," I say, then I flip up the hasp on the front of the box and lift the lid.

The cold had already fled from my bones, but at the sight of the items inside, something else releases, the last of the pressure in my chest I didn't realize was still weighing me down until it was gone.

"You motherfuckers," I say, pulling my missing tarot cards out of the box as a smile creeps up my face. The Moon and the Four of Swords stare—insomuch as something without even the image of eyes on it can stare—up at me cheekily. I set them on my lap and start digging through the rest. Movie tickets from nights out with Aaron. Battered bookmarks that should have been inside keeping my place. My favorite pen (nothing I've encountered in all my years so far writes as smoothly). My favorite sewing needle, wrapped with my go-to mending thread.

I still have to get to the library to help clean up. I still have to go to work and figure out my new job. I still have to call my parents and apologize again, tell them I love them, and work on building up all the trust I lost with them and my friends.

But in this moment, with what feels like whole chunks of my life found, I think it's all going to be okay.

There's just one other person I have to apologize to.

I push all the other knickknacks to the side and look straight down into the bottom of the box.

"Hey, you. Sorry it took me so long." I smile down into the little rectangular mirror glued to the bottom, scratched and smudged but clear enough for me to see my own face reflected in it, the sun shining through my lashes for the first time in ages. "I missed you."

Preview the next book in
A HORDE OF DEAD POETS
collection!

AVAILABLE NOW

One

Chloe couldn't wait to continue the massacre. She wanted to rip its mouth open and peel back each layer until it was stripped bare. After all, a house was not a house without a good set of bones.

Driving up the spindly two-lane highway, Chloe's mind spun as she eagerly looked out the passenger side window of their crossover SUV. After driving a little over four hours toward the Sierra Nevada, the sky brightened to blue, instead of the depressing gray Bay Area smog disguising itself as a marine layer. Giant pine trees replaced skyscrapers and congested traffic. Chloe rolled her window down and inhaled. Petrichor laced the mountain air. She relished the earthy scent with another long inhale as she noticed pools of water collecting in the rich, copper soil. They passed a large, carved wooden sign with bold letters stating, "Hallowed Pines, Population 327." Thick vines of poison oak wrapped around the sign's wooden posts, their familiar shade pricking her mind. Chloe sat up in her seat.

The swatches.

"I forgot to show you," Chloe said, shuffling around in her messenger bag. She pulled out a three-ring binder full of color tabs and fabric samples. "I found *the* perfect wallpaper for the living room. It's a beautiful woodland baroque-style design that will go well with the wainscotting. I got confirmation that it was delivered to the house last week, so we can put it up right away. Here, take a quick look."

Philip peeled his gaze off the road. "Wow, that's gorgeous. You really have a great eye for design, babe."

Chloe smoothed the patch of wallpaper in her binder. "The building has been vacant for so long. I'm sure it will welcome a new set of skin. The living room has enough space for a bold pattern. I don't think we'll have any problem reaching a perfect kill point."

Philip sighed. "You always have to be so morbid, don't you?"

"Hey, that's what they call it in the interior design world." Chloe closed her home décor binder and turned to face him. "The kill point is where the first and final pieces of wallpaper meet."

"Ah, yes," he replied with a nod. "The 'new skin,' right?"

She nudged his arm with her elbow. "It adds some personality to the home. You know, in some cultures, people talk to their houses. Some even give it a name."

"I see." Philip scratched the bridge of his nose underneath his wire-framed glasses before flipping up the sun visor. "So, it turns out I'm not the only practicing physician after all, what with you tending to buildings like I do to patients."

Chloe smirked as she adjusted her seatbelt. "Physician? No, my four years of design school don't compare with your hard work, Dr. Blackwell." She swallowed the sour tang of her parents' words. "If only my parents would be proud that I'm finally putting my degree to use."

Philip reached over, sliding his hand underneath hers. Intertwining their fingers, he lifted her hand to his lips. "You always make me proud," he whispered and kissed her skin.

Proud. A word so foreign to Chloe. She considered her parents to be bilingual—fluent in sarcasm and criticism. *Focus on math instead of art, dear,* they'd told her in elementary school. *What good is an interior design degree in today's market,* her father questioned her at her college graduation dinner. *He's too mature for you,* they said after meeting Philip for the first time. *His on-call hospital shifts will be the death of your marriage,* her mother warned when Chloe shared the news of their engagement. Chloe was convinced her parents drank her tears like a fine wine, savoring every drop of sadness. She had given up trying to figure them out a long time ago, but spending twenty-four years in her parents' household had taught her two things: Pain is inevitable and survival is beauty.

Now, with her hand cradled in her fiancé's, Chloe grinned and thought, *Fuck them and what they think of me. They aren't invited to the wedding anyway.*

"I love you," Chloe said, giving Philip's hand a gentle squeeze.

"I love you too." Philip returned the action, then let go of her hand. He settled his grip back on the steering wheel. "Hey, can you crack open a bottle of water for me? I swear, this mountain air always makes my allergies flare up."

Chloe reached down and twisted the cap off a water bottle. "What? You already miss the Bay Area pollution? I thought the mountain air was better for your lungs."

"You know what I mean," Philip said as he playfully swiped the bottle from Chloe's grasp.

Chloe watched as he tilted his head back, appreciating him. Philip was the type of person who seemed to be born in the wrong era. Sure, he was twelve years older than her, but Chloe didn't mind the age gap. She admired his chiseled jawline under his dark brown five o'clock shadow. She enjoyed the way he brushed his wavy brown hair back, exposing his receding hairline. He was romantic, preferred phone conversations instead of text messages, enjoyed home-cooked meals over racking up Uber Eats rewards, and above all else, he was always willing to help others.

A gentle warmth bloomed inside her as she recalled meeting Philip for the first time. After Chloe had sliced her hand on a broken wine glass in a crowded San Francisco bar, Philip ushered her safely to his apartment less than a block away to tend to her wound so she could avoid a hefty emergency room bill. Maybe it wasn't love at first sight, but it was love at first stitch and that was enough for her.

Chloe smoothed the hem of her sweater. "Do you think your parents are going to be able to stop by the house while we're here? I'd love for them to see all the work we've done on the place."

"Shoot, I forgot to tell you," Philip replied shaking his head. "They took a last-minute trip to South Carolina to help a church family in expediting their tiny home operation before the summer heat starts."

"South Carolina?" Chloe asked, twirling a chunk of her hair around her finger. "Why so far?"

"It's part of some ministry," he explained. "They've been helping installing tiny homes, creating a positive community for the homeless. I guess there are about twenty families ready to move in, so a member of the east-coast chapter congregation asked for volunteers. But don't worry, they'll be back in time for the wedding next month."

"Oh, that's so kind of them," Chloe said with a lopsided smile. She had only met Philip's parents twice before, and she couldn't gauge whether his parents considered her worthy enough to become part of the family. Philip admitted he prayed every now and then, but he left most of his religious practices and beliefs behind after moving to the city for college. The closest Chloe ever came to being considered religious was when she cried out to God while in bed with Philip. "You don't think they're still upset that we're converting your family's old church into a house?"

"What?" Philip glanced at her and then steadied his eyes on the road. "Of course not. They are happy someone in the family is doing something with it. My younger brother is too busy traveling in New Zealand, and my older sister is in Tennessee. So, really, it's kind of fallen on my shoulders since I'm the only child still in California. But after they see what we do, how *you're* going to work your incredible magic on the inside, I have no doubt all of them will be proud of us."

Proud. That word again. Chloe twisted in her seat as butterflies took flight in her stomach. "And they liked your idea of us putting it on the market after the wedding, right?"

Philip snapped his lips closed. He cleared his throat, reaching for his drink in the cup holder.

"Babe"—Chloe watched him rush the water bottle to his mouth—"please tell me you told them we aren't moving out of the city."

Philip swallowed hard, choking on the last sip. "I—I will."

"Philip," Chloe cursed and turned off the radio. "You

were supposed to tell them our plan. Wait, you're not having second thoughts, are you?"

"No," Philip said, locking eyes with her. "Of course not. Our lives are in the Bay Area. They get that. I just haven't fully told them we intend to sell this place so we can buy a home in the city. It's not going to be easy for them to say goodbye to the property that's been in my family's name for four generations."

Chloe placed her hands in her lap as her heart sank. Not only did she worry about what Philip's parents were going to say when they heard the news, but she also worried about what kind of wedge this was going to drive into their relationship. Announcing their quick engagement had been a shock, nothing a little time couldn't heal. But this? This had the potential to be as catastrophic as an earthquake tearing the Bay Bridge in two.

Chloe parted her lips, an apology forming on her tongue. But a dark figure flashed in her peripheral vision.

Time slowed as she peeled her gaze from Philip. Two black eyes locked onto hers. Chloe's heartbeat pounded against her eardrums. Adrenaline shot through her veins, piercing every inch of her skin.

"Philip!" she shouted and pointed to the windshield.

He turned his attention back to the road. The brakes squealed as Philip twisted the steering wheel to the left. The deer ran across the roadway, becoming a blur of brown. Their tires swerved over the double yellow line as Philip tried to slow the car. A fawn leaped over the hillside. Its legs scrambled against the asphalt as it tried to catch up to its mother across the road. Chloe screamed as she gripped the door handle, bracing herself.

Metal crunched upon impact. The left side of the car

lurched up and forward as the tires rolled over something large. A loud pop erupted.

"Shit," Philip said with a huff. "Oh my god, Chloe. Are you okay?"

She slowly opened her eyes. Dust swirled in the air, curling around the raised corner of the SUV hood. She exhaled in relief at seeing the dashboard still intact.

Her arms burned with the electricity of adrenaline. Her lower lip trembled. She unlocked her death grip on the handle. A throbbing pain pulsed at her hairline. She wiped her hair back, examining her fingertips. Not a drop of blood appeared on her skin. Relief that they hadn't hit the full-grown deer flooded through her, but *oh god*, the baby.

"I'm okay," she responded through a shaky breath.

"Good," Philip murmured. He pried his hands from the steering wheel and turned the ignition. The idling engine stopped. Reaching over, he smoothed her hair back. His fingers traced along the back of her neck as he gently pressed into her skin, examining her.

Chloe's chest tightened. "Oh god, the deer." She turned toward Philip in her seat. Tears pooled against her eyelids. "Is it..."

"Dead." Philip swallowed hard. "At least I hope it is."

Chloe dabbed a sore spot forming on her forehead. Glancing down, she noticed the splatter of colors across her lap. The accident had caused her décor binder to spew paint swatches, magazine clippings, and fabric samples everywhere. But she was still alive.

"What should we do?"

Philip sucked in a breath as he pulled back her hair from her face. His fingers brushed against her skin as his eyes searched her face. "No sign of bleeding. Pupils are equal, round, and reactive. Neck is—"

"Hey," Chloe said, pulling away from his touch. "I'm fine. No need to dictate a full examination."

"It's what I do," he admitted. "I need to know you're okay."

A car honked twice from behind them, stealing their attention. Chloe checked the passenger side mirror. An oversized red truck pulled off the road and parked behind their SUV.

"Thank the Lord," Philip murmured.

Chloe followed Philip as they both carefully got out of their vehicle. The diesel engine rattled the air before the driver killed it. She rounded the rear side of their SUV but stopped at the sight of the fawn behind their car.

Blood pooled underneath the fawn's carcass. Its head twisted to the side, its neck stretching like warped putty. Chloe winced as her stomach churned. Its lifeless eyes remained open, searching for the afterlife.

"Oh god." Chloe choked back a sob.

Philip rounded the SUV, approaching her with open arms. "It's okay. Shh, it's okay."

Chloe rested her head against his chest. The oak scent of Philip's cologne grounded her. Things could've been worse.

"Just an accident," he whispered into her hair.

She wiped her tears against his shirt. "It was so young."

He rubbed her back and tried to quiet her worries. "I didn't mean to hit it." Philip's chest rose and fell as he let out a heavy breath. "And death isn't ageist."

Chloe pressed her hand against his chest, breaking their embrace. She searched his eyes, taken aback by his matter-of-fact attitude. But of course he would need to compartmentalize death; he was a doctor.

"Holy spit!" A man climbed out of the cab of his red truck. "That som'a bitch jumped out right in front of ya." He had a beard as thick as the forest and he shuffled toward them.

Philip walked away from Chloe and met the man between the cars. Their hands collided, clasping together in a firm shake.

"I tried to dodge it," Philip explained. "You'd think I wasn't raised up here with those things crossing the road all the time."

"Livin' down in those cities will do that to ya, Philly," the man said. In a town of only a few hundred people, of course Philip knew the man. He nodded his chin toward Chloe. "Miss, are ya okay?"

"I'm fine," she replied. "Just a little on edge."

"Rusty, this is my fiancée, Chloe," Philip explained.

The old man smoothed his beard. "Welcome to Hallowed Pines. Nice to meet ya."

Chloe forced a smile, still tense from the accident. She rested her hip on the side of their car. "What should we do? Call the police?"

The older man barked out a laugh. "Oh, I'm afraid that's not going to be helpful, seeing as the closest law enforcement office is more than thirty minutes away."

Chloe cocked her head and flashed a concerned look at Philip.

He acknowledged her with a nod. "Rusty, what about the fire department?"

The old man adjusted his belt. "You mean the one that got shut down two years ago? We've only got a few of us who volunteer up here and you're lookin' at one of 'em right now."

A chill snaked down Chloe's spine. The lack of resources in a town nestled in the forest forced her to consider the overall remoteness of the area. There was no way in hell she could ever live like this.

Rusty waved at an incoming car as he and Philip discussed their car's damage. She drowned out most of their conversation, catching only pieces: something about their alignment being off; the bumper needing some-such repair; a cracked headlight lens. She glanced at the young deer. This poor animal died, never to roam the forest again. Guilt pooled in her center. *All because I distracted Philip's driving.* Bile climbed up her throat as her stomach knotted. "I think I'm just going to walk the rest of the way."

Philip broke away from his conversation with Rusty. "Sweetie, are you sure? I don't know if it's a good idea for you to be al—"

"I told you that I'm fine," Chloe assured him. She pointed toward the road. "It's not that far. Just a five-minute walk or so. The fresh air would be good."

Philip pressed his forehead against hers as he embraced her. "Okay. Just be careful. I can't let anything happen to you," he whispered.

She eased into his arms, not caring if the other man was watching. Philip loved her deeply and wanted her to be safe, no matter where she went. His desire to protect her at all times added another layer to their love. Another month and he would be vowing his life to her and she to him.

"I'll text you when I'm there," she said, pulling away from him.

She returned to the car and collected her cell phone and

purse. She glanced at the mess of her binder. She could fix that later. Right now, she wanted to get far away from the scene of the accident and shed the guilt that gnawed at her. Her new wallpaper was waiting.

She waved to the two men and set off. Their voices grew distant as Chloe walked along the side of the road. The sound of crunching pine needles underneath her sneakers became the rustic soundtrack to her journey. She breathed in the mountain air and smiled. At least she was getting her steps in.

As the road stretched and veered to the right, Chloe ventured down a beaten path. Gravel crunched under her shoes as she picked up her pace. As she walked down the private driveway, the silhouette of the steeple poked through the pine tree canopy. She passed a sun-bleached wooden sign that read "Hallowed Pines Gathering," the name of the former church Philip's family founded. The first time Philip brought her to Hallowed Pines, Chloe had joked that the name sounded more like a cult, than an evangelical church. The fact that the prior congregation only had thirty members provided further suspicions of what exactly when on in the building. Philip explained that their church had been different. That his grandfather's mission had been to create a *movement.*

"Like a former secret society," Chloe had laughed at the explanation, but Philip's stern look drained any suggestion that he was joking. And she'd been too nervous, and a little creeped out, to ask any more questions.

As the building came into full view, Chloe's heart brightened. She couldn't tell why, but when Philip first showed her the property, Chloe felt an immense fascination. Built in the 1930s, the roughly 1200-square foot building sat centered on the 20-acre plot of dense forestry. *A hidden gem,* she'd told Philip on her first visit. She valued the vacant space for its potential. An opportunity to showcase her craft of revitalizing the forgotten into something memorable. Determined, Chloe was set to transform this former church into a wonderful ranch-style home.

As Chloe stepped onto the porch, the scent of fresh paint greeted her. She cocked her head, examining how the sunlight illuminated the new shiplap walls. The color turned out to be more yellow than she had intended. Her chest pinched, wishing she could have confirmed the painters had used the right hue.

Fuck it, Chloe thought. *It's close enough.*

She fumbled through her purse and pulled out a set of keys. Reaching for the doorknob, she froze. Fear pricked the back of her neck, tugging her back a step.

The front door swung open on its own.

ENJOY THESE NOVELLAS IN ANY ORDER!

A HORDE OF DEAD POETS
A BETTER GRAVE THAN THIS
JESSICA CRANBERRY

A HORDE OF DEAD POETS
SOME RAIN MUST FALL
MEG DAILEY

A HORDE OF DEAD POETS
SUCH GOOD BONES
LENN WOOLSTON

A HORDE OF DEAD POETS
IN THE HAUNTS OF GOBLIN MEN
CANDACE ROBINSON
S.G.D. SINGH

A HORDE OF DEAD POETS
DEATH'S MAIDEN
ELLE BEAUMONT

A HORDE OF DEAD POETS
DESCENDANTS OF THE BIG HOUSE
C. VONZALE LEWIS

A HORDE OF DEAD POETS

Acknowledgments

Oh, man. Of all the parts of writing A Thing, this was the part I was most dreading. What if I forget someone? But also, anyone who knows me knows my memory is awful, so if you're feeling left out, know it wasn't intentional. I still appreciate you!

I'll start with my family: Mom and Dad, Aunt Sissy, and Grammy, all of whom continue to support my love of books and my interest in writing, even if it takes a mortal age to get anything written. Thank you all for your patience. The teleportation machine is still on The List.

Next, my closest friends and stalwart D&D group: Regina, Stacey, Matt, Katie, and Dan. Thank you all for being the creative, hilarious, wonderful people that you are. Sorry I asked a bunch of you to beta-read this and then procrastinated so hard that there wasn't time. I hope normal-reading it will be just as fun!

Many thanks too to the awesome group at Midnight Tide Publishing, especially Lou Wilham, fabulous writing coach and cheerleader, who has way more confidence in my ability to make the words go than I ever will. And of course, Jess and Carla of Percy's Heart Press, who invited me to join in on this collection and provided amazing feedback and suggestions to whip this story into shape. I continue to be honored to be among such fine authors!

Finally, my biggest supporter and love of my life, Richard. Thank you for always being there for me, or being in the next room when "there" is a place I need to be alone. We should, like, get married and raise a couple stupid cats together or something.

About Meg Dailey

Meg has been editing independently for more than 10 years. She's been a member of the Editorial Freelancers Association since 2017 and spent two years as Lead Editor of Anthologies with a small-press publisher. She is now an affiliate editor for the growing co-op Midnight Tide Publishing.

She's an avid reader, self-diagnosed YA addict, and strong believer in the NA genre. Her TBR is ever-growing.

She also writes! Just . . . very slowly . . .

 instagram.com/thedaileyeditor

Also by Meg Dailey

Anthologies

Masks (foreword)

Emporium of Superstition

The Darkest Lullaby (foreword)